Rosemary's Rhapsody
by
Marcella Taylor Hoffman

Third in the series
Hearts in Harmony
The Alverson Family Saga

THIS BOOK BELONGS TO:
Clayton Gospel Church
2045 Highway 87 South
Clayton, NM 88415

<u>Rosemary's Rhapsody</u>
by Marcella Taylor Hoffman
ISBN No. 0-9774324-6-7
Library of Congress No. 2012949385
Copyright© by Marcella Shugars
December, 2012

Although the author and publisher have made every effort to ensure the accuracy and completeness of information contained in the book, we assume no responsibility for errors, inaccuracies omissions, or any inconsistency herein. Any slights of people, places or organizations are unintentional.

This book is a work of fiction. Although influenced by a variety of personalities the author has observed, no character is patterned after any single individual or meant to portray any real person. All names, places and events are either used fictionally or are products of the author's imagination.

All rights reserved. No part of this publication may be reproduced or transmitted in any form or by any means without written permission of the author.

Cover: Graphics by Tara Berguis,
TaraJoy Designs
Photographic images provided by the author

Published by Golden Apple Greetings
5066 Lake Michigan Drive, Allendale, MI 49401
<u>www.goldenapplegreetings.com</u>

Marcella Taylor Hoffman

is now Mrs. Bert Shugars. She lives in Hartford, Michigan. She has been writing "practice novels" since she was in high school, but did not become a serious writer until, as a grandmother, she began to write inspirational novels, like *Valley of Hope* and *Caravan West*, which evolved into the Hearts in Harmony series.

Seeing that writing talent had been passed down to the next two generations, she wanted to set a good example by using her God-given talent to touch lives and illustrate a specific Christian principle in each book.

Dedication

I want to thank my family for encouragement, and give special thanks to my daughter, Sherry Kuyt, who worked tirelessly while editing this series, questioning details and time lines in a way that only another writer could do, until it all flowed together smoothly.

These books are dedicated to my family, especially my children Sherry, Clifford, Susan and Eric; and my sister Jeanne.

There he is at last!

I nearly cried out in excitement! His searching eyes lit up when they found me. His scarred lip trembled, and seconds later he had gathered me in his arms. There was a long, warm kiss, right there in the airport, and then a moment of laughter because we both had tears in our eyes. Hand in hand, we went to retrieve his luggage and headed out to the parking lot.

(from Rosemary's Rhapsody)

It's going to be a very long trip; it might take us a week or more, depending on how the bus holds up.

by Rosemary H., 1946

PROLOGUE

The story in my previous books about the Alversons began before I was even born, but as I kept journals of the memories that my mama, Matilda, shared with us, I began using my own imagination to fill in large gaps in time. It could have happened that way.

In this book, and the one following, I continue the story from my own viewpoint. I will let my faithful readers decide whether the story I have woven has touched hearts and illustrated values that many other large Christian families would like to pass on as well.

Rosemary Alverson *

fictional narrator

"...a three-story Spanish hacienda with boarded-up shutters and a lettered sign spelling out ALVERSON INN."

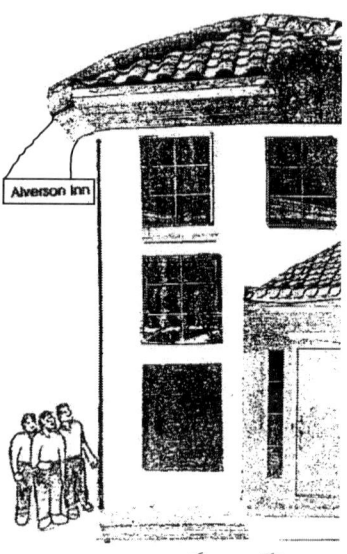

by Rosemary A., 1946

CHAPTER 1

It was still broad daylight on that hot summer evening in 1946, and humid.

I lay in bed glowering at my sister's ticking clock, not because it made too much noise or anything. It just seemed to mock me, because here I was almost eleven years old and hustled off to bed at eight o'clock for no good reason, with school being out and all.

Margaret would not come up for hours; in fact, the whole family got to stay up except my brother Tory and me. They were all outdoors now, making so much racket outside my open window I couldn't sleep if I wanted to.

Incredibly bored, I entertained myself by winding a brown pigtail around one of the bars in my iron bed frame, thinking how much they resembled prison bars. Well, I may as well be in jail, being forced to suffer up here all alone.

I stared at the pale pink wallpaper. Too much pink in this room. I had wanted yellow.

My 19-year-old sister, Margaret, had been

allowed to choose the color – even new pink flowered curtains and a matching skirt for her vanity dresser, all because she had earned the money herself. Her oval-shaped looking glass, with its gilded frame, seemed out of place with the old bed and dresser we shared. I crept out of bed to sit on her vanity stool and examine the things I was never allowed to touch.

There was a decorated comb and brush set; scarlet lipstick; leg makeup; and an eye-brow pencil that she used to paint seam lines on the back of her legs, like real silk stockings. The large photograph of Derron Powell, Margaret's fiancé, that she mooned over every evening. Then Margaret's graduation photo in a golden frame caught my eye, and I looked at my own reflection now, for comparison.

My teeth were definitely too wide and my eyebrows too thick. My elbows were knobby like my knees, and my "nightie" was actually my brother Tim's old V-neck tee shirt, baggy at the shoulders and hanging well below my own under garment.

Rosemary Alverson, I asked the awkward girl in the mirror, will you ever grow out of this gawky stage and look anything like your three pretty sisters? I wondered if any handsome man would ever fall in love with me, and want to marry me.

Then, what sounded like a two-ton truck outside

began chugging and sputtering away, so near that it drowned out all the shouting now, then stopped and started again. I couldn't resist getting up and tiptoeing into the boys' room, where its big windows faced Elm Street.

I pushed aside the plastic drapes, and there it sat, parked in front of our house – the longest, oldest bus I had ever seen. And the man at the wheel was ... my father!

I must be dreaming. My Daddy wasn't a bus driver! He made his living washing and drying other people's clothes at the Clark Street Laundry & Cleaners, here in Urbandale, Michigan. He came home every day with white blotches all over his raggedy work clothes, from bleach that splattered when he loaded the giant wash machines by himself. I felt guilty when I remembered my shame over him one day, when he picked me up at my new friend's birthday party. I was younger then. That was before I had even asked Jesus to come into my heart. So I did not understand, yet, that my hard-working parents were a precious gift from God.

Sitting cross-legged on the boys' cracked linoleum, I leaned against the windowsill and thought about this while I watched and wondered.

My Mama worked there at the laundry, too, as a wool presser; and my two older brothers even worked there in the summer, emptying pockets and sorting the mountains of dirty clothes before Daddy stuffed them into net bags and hauled them up for the first wash cycle.

Did Daddy plan on changing jobs? Does a bus driver earn more money than a laundry man?

I did hear my parents say once that his company didn't pay him enough money for his heavy job. Margaret made much more on the assembly line at GM, they said, until the war ended and they laid her off. But Mama said it was the best job Daddy could get without an education, and steady. He had never reached high school because his family had moved so much.

"That's why he hates to travel now," Mama once told us, "even to visit out-of-town relatives."

Just a few months ago, Daddy had turned down Mama's suggestion that they all make a trip to Ann Arbor this summer, to see Uncle Tommy and Aunt Lou.

"Who can afford to travel these days, Matilda? Gasoline may not be rationed anymore, but it costs a fortune! Seventeen cents a gallon, now, and going up! Besides, you don't know what hardship is until you've been stranded in the middle of nowhere like my family was long ago. It's better to find a good place and stay put, I always say!"

We all knew he never did get back in school, after his parents finally settled in Missouri. And, then, after his father's stroke, his mother needed the income he earned as a bellhop in the St. Louis Hotel.

My brother Tory stirred in his bed on the far end of the room, but did not wake up. How he could sleep through the terrible roar of that bus motor, I could not imagine.

Nor could I imagine Daddy as a twelve-year-old bellhop, whatever that was. All I remembered him saying about that job was that when he brought home a stack of dollar bills to his mother each month, he kept back a few until he'd saved enough to buy a brand-new bicycle; then he used this to pick up packages for hotel customers. But one day he left his bike in the alley behind the drug store, and when he came out, it was gone!

Now, in 1946, Ted Alverson, Jr. was a balding man of 43, raising his eight children with "the sweetest woman God could have provided!" They had survived the Great Depression together, and my Mama had recovered from a long illness; yet they were still barely managing to pay rent and feed and clothe their family. But there he was, coming home with that monstrous vehicle and beaming every bit as though it belonged to him!

The motor stopped now, and the cheering and

clapping began anew. I couldn't see everybody because the porch roof blocked my view; but, from the sound of their voices, Mama and the girls must be on the front porch. Tom, Teddy Cooper and Tim stood around on the sidewalk with their thumbs hooked in their overall pockets, listening to a tall stranger tell Daddy what a bargain he was getting for a song.

I ran to get Margaret's bathrobe and put it on. On her it just covered her knees; on me it dragged on the floor. I had to be careful not to trip, but I couldn't resist hurrying down the stairs now, knowing Mama would scold me, but determined to find out why my Daddy would buy a bus. The last I knew, he could barely afford to buy a gallon of gasoline for the Chevy and take us to church.

By the time I got down there, the tall stranger was driving away with another man – in our car! Daddy had already let the boys clamber onto the bus and take seats behind him. He called to Mama, "Matilda, I'm gonna take another spin around the block!"

Mama nodded and waved, and when she noticed me standing there, she gave me a hug. She wasn't even mad at me for getting up. In fact, even 9-year-old Tory was up now, and had run outside, just in time for Daddy to let him come along for the ride.

"We just wanted a chance to talk to the man, Rosie, without so many young kids around," she said. "You can stay up for awhile now, if you want to. We're gonna have some ice cream and cookies."

Ice cream? We never had ice cream, except for birthdays, and mine was still almost two weeks away!

Why was Mama so cheerful? Something had taken years of worry from her face.

Mama opened the screen door and went inside. Then I asked Margaret, "Why is Daddy buying a bus?"

"Why are you wearing my bathrobe?"

My sisters all looked at each other and giggled, and I followed them into the house. "Ask Mama," Margaret told me. "She'll explain it all."

Daddy and the boys were back, now, and I watched Mama cutting the quart of ice cream into ten thin slices.

"What does she mean, Mama?"

She smiled at me. "Eat your ice cream, Honey. Then we'll talk."

"Pretty good riding for an old clunker, Matilda," Daddy announced as he came in the door. "Just needs one window replaced, and a little mending on some of the seats. And those tires won't last the whole trip. I 'spect I'd better look for some spares with a little more tread on them."

"Trip? What trip, Daddy?"

He just grinned. I finished my ice cream, and Mama said, "We'll go upstairs now, and talk about it."

Mama usually talked to us all at once, or to whoever happened to be in the room. This must be pretty special, for her to follow me all the way upstairs and talk just to me.

"We didn't want to tell all of you kids until we were sure," she began. She sat next to me on the bed and seemed to be having a hard time getting the words out.

"We're going to be moving soon, Rosemary."

"Moving? Moving where?"

"Away from Urbandale."

"But why? Daddy always says, 'Find a good place and stay put!'"

"Well, sometimes things change, and we have to make changes to allow for them."

I still didn't understand.

"Do you remember, a couple of months ago, when Daddy got a telegram from Uncle Tommy, in Ann Arbor?"

"You mean when their Grandmother died?"

She nodded. "Do you remember how Daddy said he couldn't have gone out West for the funeral, even if he had gas money, because it was already over by the time he heard about it?"

"I remember. He went to visit Uncle Tommy by himself, though, right? Are we moving to Ann Arbor to be near relatives?"

I barely remembered Uncle Tommy and Aunt Lou, from the time we took a Greyhound bus trip to visit them, while the big kids went to camp. I was only six years old then, and Tory was four.

Uncle Tommy looked a lot like our Daddy, but he was taller and had curlier hair. Aunt Lou combed her dark hair straight back and pinned it up in a bun on the back of her head.

I remembered how Uncle Tommy always said "'Nother words" after he told you something, and then told you again. I remembered that they lived in an adobe block house that Uncle Tommy built himself. There were no walls dividing the rooms - only sheets hung on wires, except where an old china cabinet and bookcase and dresser separated the parents' sleeping area from the children's.

Tommy worked for a bottle factory nearby; but they seemed even poorer than we were! They had seven children then, and another on the way. And another baby was born since then, Mama told us, so that made nine in all. We only had eight.

Most of all, I remembered they sang the same

prayer at the table that we always sang at home, before supper:

Be present at our table, Lord;
Be here and everywhere adored;
Thy creatures bless, and grant that we
May feast in paradise with thee.

They also got their musical instruments out as soon as Sunday dinner dishes were done, just like my parents sometimes did at home, and sang old-time gospel songs. This had been the highlight of our visit. It was like – like a rhapsody when they played and sang together.

I liked the word, rhapsody. It was one of my spelling words last year. My teacher said it was a type of song, but it also meant "joy." Whenever I saw the happy faces of my family as they made music together, I thought of that beautiful word.

I had not seen Uncle Tommy and Aunt Lou since then. Aunt Molly and Uncle Howard came to visit us sometimes, but travel was too expensive for most people, Daddy said. We just wrote letters.

Mama went on talking, bringing me back to the present. "Do you know what Daddy went to see his brother about?"

"Not exactly."

"Well," she said. "We didn't know until after Grandma and Grandpa died a while back that Grandpa Ted's mother was still living, in New Mexico. That would be your great-grandmother, Elizabeth Alverson."

"So, Daddy is Ted Alverson, Jr., right? And Teddy Cooper is ..."

"Ted Alverson the third. A lot of the children are named after one of the ancestors, and the boys' names usually start with a T. We named him Teddy Cooper after a man who owned the farm we lived on in St. Louis."

Such a long story! I fingered the small yellow square that had worn loose in the summer quilt I used as a bedspread.

"Anyway," she went on, "Grandpa Ted was Elizabeth's oldest son. I've been told that both of his parents were disappointed in him for something he did a long time ago. Especially his father, Thurmond. So, Grandpa Ted never wrote to them or saw them again in all those years. He didn't even talk about them. As a result, Elizabeth didn't even know when he and Grandma Ellen died in the accident.

"Still, his mother thought of him often. After his father died, she started trying to locate him, but didn't know where to begin. Finally, as a 96-year-old widow, she learned the whereabouts of one of Ted's sons – your Uncle Tommy. Her attorney finally tracked him down in Michigan, and she wrote to him, but it was too late."

Mama shook her head slowly. "She died the day before his letter of response arrived. When Tommy received news of her passing away, he sent out telegrams to your Daddy and their two sisters."

I couldn't help fidgeting, although I knew it wasn't polite.

"Oh, I know it's complicated, Dear. But, I'm telling you this because Daddy's grandmother left him something in her will."

That got my attention. "You mean, she left him some money?"

"Well, yes. But it has some strings attached. Each of Grandpa Ted's children gets $25,000 - but only if they move to Chaparral, New Mexico, where Daddy lived as a little boy. There is a house there for each family, too, and part interest in a much larger house that Grandma Elizabeth wanted to turn into a hotel."

I put my hand over my mouth to keep from screaming. Even I knew that, in 1946, you could buy four or five houses like the one we lived in for that much money.

"So Daddy's going to drive us there in a bus?"

"That's right. And, it's going to be a very long trip; it might take us a week or more, depending on how the bus holds out."

"When will we leave?"

"At the end of this month. Tommy and Lou will be meeting us here, along with Molly and Vera and their families, and we'll all travel to New Mexico together. The Alverson Inn will be a family-run business."

All of those people Mama told stories about, whenever a letter came that got her thinking about them! They were coming here?

"You mean our cousins will come along? Betsey and Tucker, and ...?"

"Yes. All of your cousins in Michigan. The ones you know, and the ones you don't know, like Aunt Vera's seven children, from Petoskey, and Uncle Tommy's nine. Even the boy who just came home from the war."

"But, not the ones in Indiana, right?"

"Right. Those are on my side of the family. Only Grandpa Ted's descendants are involved. Now, you go and wait your turn for the outhouse, and then get to bed. Tomorrow, we'll have to start packing!"

***

I still lay awake when Margaret came to bed, and long after I heard her sleeping soundly.

Questions swam around in my head until I thought I would drown in confusion.

What will it be like to leave home and travel across the country by bus? Will my other cousins be as friendly as Betsey and Tucker, whom I see almost every summer?

As I drifted off to sleep, another question was going through my mind. What could Grandpa Ted have done to make his father so upset with him?

CHAPTER 2

I woke up hearing Mama down in the kitchen with that lilt in her voice, like it sometimes had on Christmas morning.

I dressed quickly and hurried down the stairs for breakfast. It felt good to hear her laughing, and see her without the worry in her eyes that had appeared so often in the past few years. Even Daddy seemed younger and more optimistic, as he scurried around the house that next few days.

"Do we have to sell the house before we move?" I asked, buttering the toast as Mama deftly put two more slices of bread into the toaster and pulled the sloping toaster doors closed.

"No," she said. "We're merely renting this house, so all we have to do is notify the landlord, then sell whatever furniture we can to raise money for the trip." She dipped hot cocoa into mugs and placed them carefully next to each plate.

"Make sure everybody's up, will you, Honey?"

But, before I even got to the foot of the stairs, two boys were coming down, and others came in from all directions. Mama flipped the last of the fried eggs onto a platter being kept warm in the oven, and then lifted out the whole platter to place in the middle of the kitchen table, with a pan of hot toast for dunking into the cocoa. Daddy came in just in time to sit down and say the blessing. Life was good in Urbandale, even though we were not rich.

Mama's cousin Peggy, from Indiana, came to visit after hearing the news and made arrangements to buy most of the furniture for her daughter, and a few pieces for herself, providing she could bring the money next payday.

"What do you think, Ted?" Mama asked him, which was unusual because he usually left it up to her to manage the money for the family.

"Just make sure we have it before we leave. We're going to need all the money we can scrape up to make this trip!"

Cousin Peggy stood with her hand still stroking the polished wooden radio cabinet, acting like it was already hers.

It was on that same radio that Mama and Daddy first heard about the market crash in 1929. Years later, they heard President Roosevelt announce that war had been declared; and then last year they heard President Truman announce that the war was over.

Us kids had listened to all of our favorite programs on that radio, and Daddy and Mama had listened to "Fibber McGee and Molly" on it too. It was old, but it worked good, and the cabinet was still in perfect condition.

"We'll be here with Floyd's truck the day before you leave," Peggy promised. "We'll pay you then."

Mama reminded Daddy to cut the boys' hair before the aunts and uncles arrived. She knew that one of the first things Molly and Howard would surely do, when we all got together, would be to line up each family and take our pictures.

Daddy set up his barbershop on the front porch and went to work, biting his tongue as he usually did when putting his best efforts into a task. Mama then cut Daddy's hair, and then assigned me the job of sweeping up all of the hair from the porch.

Some of the Elm Street neighbors could be seen staring from their windows while Daddy worked on the bus. But, what really brought them all out to watch was when Tommy's own old bus drove up by our house ten days later, and 11 people climbed out.

Our neighbors probably never saw so many hugs or heard such joyful greetings coming from one place, especially when Daddy's sisters began to arrive with their families.

Aunt Molly, a short, wild-eyed lady, had passed her flame-red hair to all three of her children – Gloria, Tucker, and Betsey. Her husband, Howard Borden, was a bald-headed man with a sophisticated mustache, who had worked as a successful accountant in a big corporation.

Daddy's youngest sister, Vera, a shy, soft-spoken lady, wore her dark auburn hair pinned back with barrettes and trailing down to her waist. She and her husband, Edmund Rawlings, had seven well-mannered children, two of which had shades of the family's red hair that came down from Elizabeth Alverson and also from Grandma Ellen's side of the family, the McDonalds.

My Daddy and his brother both had medium brown hair like their father, and dark bushy eyebrows over deep brown eyes. But they and their sisters all shared facial expressions that made them look like Grandpa Thurmond, whose picture I had seen in our album.

That day, neighbor kids hung on their side of the fences as Uncle Tommy brought two orange circus tents out of his bus, and the other men helped put them up in our back yard.

"Why don't you kids find another place to visit right now?" my Daddy told us. "Give us some room to work. You can come and look at the tents when we're done."

"Just think," Margaret said, as we came around the house to sit on the front porch with several of our cousins. "This is the way we're going to travel! We'll be camping every night in a different spot."

Tommy's son, Trace, who had recently come home from the Army, greeted us all, but talked mostly to Margaret. They had played together years ago when they lived at Country Haven during the depression, before I was born. I had often heard stories of how everyone had worked together there, when money was even scarcer than it was now.

"If you think we're attracting a lot of attention getting ready for this convoy, remember that our great-grandparents and their family made the same trip by covered wagon," he said. "I imagine that raised some eyebrows in Kansas City and St. Louis. I mean, that kind of transportation was common in the 1800s; but in 1906, when the Alversons went to claim New Mexico land, most people traveled by train."

"Yes, that's what my Daddy said," Margaret

agreed. "Only one of his uncles rode in the cattle train, with their best livestock and some furniture. Everybody else followed in the wagons. That must have been a long, long ride."

"Several months, I think."

"Wow!" I said. "Did they sleep in tents, too, like we're going to?"

"I think some slept in the wagons, and some on the ground, under the stars," Trace replied. "A lot of the women and young folks chose to walk most of the time, instead of being cooped up in those stuffy covered wagons. Most of the roads were in bad shape, and it gave them a pretty bumpy ride."

"They walked? How could they keep up with the horses?"

"They didn't drive their horses very hard or fast. They depended on their animals to get them two thousand miles across some rough country, so they took good care of them. Some of the men rode horseback, in front or in back of the group, to keep an eye on things. One or two might ride up ahead, so they could scout for river crossings, or the best camping places."

"Our dads were on that trip, weren't they?" I said. "But they were just little kids. How many people went with them that time? Did they have a lot of wagons?"

Trace laughed at me. "So many questions! Well, let's see. Thurmond and Elizabeth had nine children. All but three or four of them were grown up, and some of them, including our grandfather, Ted, were married and had children of their own. At least two dozen people in all, I guess, and each family had its own wagon. Probably six covered wagons."

"Jeepers!" I said, and looked at my sister, who seemed to have something else on her mind.

Margaret kept staring at Trace, as though she found it hard to believe that this grown-up man was the same little boy she had played in the sandbox with all those years ago.

Mama had once told me about the time she heard Margaret, Trace, and Virginia arguing about who owned that sandbox – the president, Mr. Cooper, or God! This reunion seemed to have brought back good memories for my sister.

"I see you're wearing an engagement ring," Trace asked Margaret now. "How does your fiancé feel about your moving across the country with your family?"

"He feels pretty good about it. He's attending a Bible school in Dallas, Texas; so this move will put me a lot closer and make visiting easier. We're getting married after he graduates next summer."

Mama called to us from the other side of the screen door. "You kids can come on in and have some lunch. We're going to eat in two shifts."

I got to sit between my favorite cousin Betsey and Uncle Tommy's daughter, Donna Jean, who was our age. Mama had made up gallons of grape Kool-Aid, and the ladies, working together in that crowded kitchen, had made platters of ground bologna sandwiches. Our kitchen chairs and dining room chairs were the same chairs. The boys had made benches by setting a board between two of them. Some of the older kids ate in the living room, balancing plates on their laps.

The adults ate last, shooing us outdoors to play on the porch or between the tents. Some of us explored inside the tents. In one of them, cots were lined up like a hospital ward. The other just had a few cots plus sleeping bags and pillows.

I couldn't believe Uncle Tommy had managed to fit so many folding cots onto his bus, plus a crib for their 14-month-old baby. My daddy, it turned out, had purchased folding beds for us, too, from the army surplus store.

Aunt Molly's family would sleep in their own travel trailer, which they would pull along for the trip. Aunt Vera and Uncle Ed would sleep in our house that night and the next night, but most of the kids would be able to sleep in the tents.

Supper was more or less the same routine – two shifts, with the adults eating first this time. Each shift said its own prayers as a group. We had roast beef and buttered corn-on-the-cob. There was more corn than beef, but it tasted good and it filled our tummies. Mama had let Betsey and I squeeze the oleo; the bags contained buttons of yellow food coloring to make it look just like real butter.

Then Mama surprised me by announcing to everyone that it would be my birthday on Saturday, and we would celebrate it today because it would be harder to serve ice cream and cake in a campground. They all sang Happy Birthday, and I blew out the eleven candles.

I thought Mama had forgotten about my

birthday, with all the excitement over the trip. But she even gave me two wrapped presents, instead of just one like I usually got. One was a nice, fat journal like the one I had admired at the dime store. The other was a large sketchpad with a pretty yellow cover, so I wouldn't have to draw all my pictures on the backs of Janet's old homework papers.

They were perfect! Mama and Daddy knew I loved to draw and write stories more than anything. I couldn't wait to find a quiet place to use my new presents. Once we were on the road, I knew I would have little time alone. But it was by far the best birthday celebration ever.

Margaret and Carrie and our cousin Caroline washed the dishes for the first shift, so there would be enough dishes for the second. Then Virginia and Mary Lou and Gloria cleaned up at the end, with the help of my Mama.

After supper, we had to use the kitchen to take our sponge baths, two or three at a time with the kitchen door closed. There was no time to fill the galvanized tub for so many people, nor to heat that much water on the stove, like we usually did for our once-a-week baths.

So, we just used water from an enameled wash pan and scrubbed all over with plenty of Ivory Soap, and water from the tea kettle, like we did every night; brushed our teeth with baking soda, then climbed into our pajamas.

We had to put our shoes back on for the trip to the outhouse, as most of us didn't have bedroom slippers. The line was longer than usual, of course, so we were ready to climb into our beds or sleeping bags as soon as we could.

The grown-ups kept telling us to hurry up, because they had lots of work to do, just getting the supplies organized and ready to pack.

The next day, excitement filled the air. We would be leaving the next day.

Daddy decided to give our bus one more coat of blue paint, and since Tommy's green bus displayed a "KILROY WAS HERE" on the back, painted in white by his second son Trent, Daddy allowed my brother Thomas to paint a "ROUTE 66" sign on the back of ours.

In the confusion of all the cousins swarming around, a porch and yard full of provisions, and men working on the buses, I hardly had a chance to examine the colorful house trailer Aunt Molly had painted. With its bright yellow, red, and blue exterior, it would be easy to recognize when we got out on the highway.

Vera and Ed's station wagon looked unusual, too. With a big load of boxes and bundles strapped on the top, I wondered if it would hold up all the way to New Mexico. Daddy said if our vehicles ever got separated in big-city traffic, it wouldn't be hard to spot any of our traveling party.

For the road, some of the rear seats had been taken out of the buses, to make room for the folded cots. Most of the other supplies and equipment had to fit into the under-bus storage compartments. We had to make good choices, leaving behind unnecessary things, but packing everything we really needed.

Each family had sold some personal items and had put the proceeds in their travel fund, along with the money from their last paychecks and their piggy banks. Mama's cousin Peggy had still not come to pay for the furniture she promised to buy.

Most of the supplies and other belongings were loaded the night before we left. Nobody had suitcases except Molly's family, who would be pulling their camper trailer at the end of our little caravan, following Vera's family in their station wagon. The rest of us used cardboard boxes and stuffed extra items into the overhead shelves, out of the way.

Before I even knew about this trip, Mama had stitched up two pairs of lightweight pajamas for each of us on her old treadle sewing machine. Then she made each of us girls flowered housecoats out of feed sacks.

When she had finished these, Mama stayed up late one night making herself some sort of sports outfit to wear on the trip. She usually wore only housedresses.

I was used to wearing hand-me-downs, but the day before all the relatives arrived, Mama bought each of us girls three pairs of dungarees – blue jeans, as my sister Margaret called them – like those she had worn to work in the defense plant. They were just like the boys' Levi's, except they zipped up on the side, not in front.

Mama also bought us striped tee-shirts to wear with the dungarees, in pretty, bright colors. These were all the rage now for pre-teens and high school girls to wear in the summer, but were also very practical for traveling and camping. We gave away most of our faded school dresses because of a shortage of space, keeping just one dress each for church. The boys received new overalls and high-top tennis shoes.

The kids were told to pack their clothes and a few personal items into two small boxes, which we marked with our names. Mama and Daddy had old duffle bags, which held two outfits each besides what they were wearing.

The aunts helped Mama go over her supply inventory the night before we left, and the girls helped to finish the packing. As items were checked off a list, they were carried out to the bus by one of the boys.

Now that the war was over, canned meat products could be readily purchased without ration stamps at our local grocery stores, if you could afford the prices. Mama and Daddy had bought 24 cans of Spam and a dozen large cans of tuna fish. Little cans of devilled ham and restaurant-size cans of meatballs and corned beef hash completed the meat supply for a week's travel with our family of ten. There were cans of pre-cooked navy beans for soup, and pork and beans. Other canned foods were Campbell's soups, evaporated milk, peas, string beans, tomatoes, peaches, applesauce, and beef stew.

Wheaties and Cream of Wheat, rice, and macaroni were added to the boxes. We packed whole-wheat flour and even a little white flour, which was hard to find and expensive – Mama said people were still hoarding it. Then corn meal went in, along with brown and white sugar (which was a treat after years of rationing) and even two boxes of confectioners sugar; some lard; baking powder and soda; real cocoa powder; and cornstarch. Spices like salt, cinnamon, pepper, and vanilla, too. I never saw so much food at once!

They packed a can of coffee and some tea bags, then a few raisins and salted nuts. Mama brought just one pound of oleo and a chunk of cheese from our own icebox. These would last a little while in the camping cooler our Daddy found at the hardware store. Half-empty containers of mustard and ketchup were tossed in – no use throwing them away, they said.

The last foods to be packed, besides our picnic lunch for the first day, were some fresh produce from our victory garden: carrots, potatoes, corn, onions, string beans, and cucumbers. Margaret had saved some money the year she worked in the factory during wartime, so she bought a bag of apples and a few oranges and lemons. She had offered to help more with the food, but Mama told her to just hang onto her nest egg unless some of it was needed on the way.

"Maybe we'll come across a produce stand," Mama said, "so we can buy some fresh berries. We might get more eggs and oleo, and hopefully some cheese and store-bought bread."

She stopped to watch the boys trying to put it all under the bus. Suddenly she began to chuckle. "With that quantity of groceries, it looks like the whole town's coming with us!"

The ladies all looked at each other and began to giggle like school girls. Now that most of the work was done, it felt good to share a companionable laugh.

"Isn't it good?" Aunt Lou said. "You know, after all these years of separation, to enjoy the warm friendship we knew during the Depression? Remember, when we were all struggling together back in St. Louis?"

Mama nodded. Yes, she remembered.

"You're sure taking a lot," Aunt Molly said, "compared to what we're bringing."

"Well, you only have three kids to feed," Mama replied, "and I figure whatever we have left we can use when we get there. We don't know for sure how soon they will come up with that inheritance money, or what might delay us on the road." She sat down on the porch railing for a few minutes to get her bearings, and then got back on her feet.

"Bring out that box of silverware, Margaret, before we end up forgetting it and have to eat with our fingers. And the oil cloth we took off the kitchen table."

"Do you have any dish towels?" Aunt Lou asked Mama. "I made up some out of flour sacks before we left, but we could use more."

"How about dish soap, and laundry soap?" Aunt Vera reminded her.

"Yes, I've got some Duz over here, and a box of Super Suds. My dishrags are not in such good shape, but I've got a big stack of them. I'm taking some bars of Ivory Soap and two bottles of shampoo. We can clean our teeth with salt water or baking soda, like we do at home."

Molly smiled at that, and nodded. "I've got a big first aid kit done up, too, in case we need it – iodine, peroxide, that sort of thing."

"And I've got stuff like pink medicine and aspirins," Aunt Lou said. "Even some Ex-Lax and Alka Seltzer. And, our daughter Virginia had some nurses training, you know."

"We'll probably each find out we forgot something, but between the four of us, we should have it covered," Mama said.

I could see that these four ladies were depending on each other for encouragement, and had mixed feelings about pulling up stakes and going into the unknown, like our ancestors did.

Once the bus itself was ready, Daddy loaded up a few tools, a lantern and fuel for it, a big car jack, and some rain gear. He placed one very important item, the family Bible, in a safe place – a compartment next to the driver's seat. Other important things were put there, including a map, an address book, and a zippered pouch of money – all that remained from his and Mama's last paychecks, plus the money they had gotten from cashing in their two war bonds.

As I watched my father working together with his brother and brothers-in-law, I realized that the men, too, would need to depend on each other in this enormous undertaking we were about to begin.

CHAPTER 3

On the day of our departure, the men loaded up the tents and folding beds while the ladies made sure all of the children were dressed, fed, and ready. Mama's Cousin Peggy came in at the last minute with the money for the furniture, and Daddy added it to his leather pouch. They lost some time because of this, having to make room for Floyd's truck to pull in and get loaded. Then Mama wanted to do a last sweeping of the bedrooms, once they were empty.

"I'm not going to leave them in a mess," she said.

Some of our young friends and playmates had bidden us goodbye the day before, but now gathered in neighboring yards to watch us go.

Mama brought out the picnic basket, and we all had to take a second look to make sure it was really her.

She was wearing a new pair of sky-blue slacks and a sporty-looking blouse that she had made from a colorful feed sack. It had a snug waist drawn in by elastic, but still looked loose and comfortable. The sleeves were rolled up like Daddy's, and her hair was tied back with a matching head scarf. This was so different from the housedresses Mama usually wore, my chin dropped, and I looked at Daddy to see if he had noticed. His eyes had widened and his eyebrows went up. He had noticed.

Mama put the picnic basket in and Daddy loaded up several jugs of water. The boys started to climb into the bus, but Daddy told them to wait. He started to try to talk over the noisy chatter, holding up his hand to signal that he wanted silence. Uncle Tommy gave a shrill whistle to get everyone's attention.

"Before we leave," Daddy called out, "let's all bow our heads in prayer."

Over the hush that followed, he prayed, "Dear Heavenly Father, we thank Thee for providing the means and the opportunity for this venture. Let us live and work in harmony wherever we are and whatever challenges we face. Give us travel mercy, Lord. Keep us safe and well and always aware of Your presence. In the name of our Savior, Jesus Christ, we pray. Amen."

Uncle Tommy led the way, backing his big green bus out onto Elm Street, and heading east. My Daddy followed with our blue bus, and both of the cars followed close behind, with Molly and Howard pulling their colorful house trailer as the tail end of this quaint-looking caravan. Daddy tooted his big horn at the waving neighbors. He had studied Tommy's map, and knew which way to go, but you could tell he wasn't really used to driving a bus.

Up until now, it had mostly seemed like an exciting dream to me, but as we turned left onto Big Jennings headed for Main Street, it suddenly became a reality that we were leaving our old neighborhood. We passed the Doornbos Market, the school, and the dry goods store, and the community library. Then we were turning left again on Main Street and heading for the highway that would take us south, toward the Michigan and Indiana border.

About twenty minutes from home, just outside of the city limits, Uncle Tommy tapped on his horn and motioned to Daddy to pull over. They pulled onto a side road not far from the highway entrance ramp, and as Daddy rolled his window down, Tommy approached on foot, looking somewhat embarrassed.

"What's up?"

"I forgot that letter with the address and directions in it, that we'll need once we get to New Mexico. I took it out of my pocket when I shaved this morning and it's not here. 'Nother words, I think I left it by your kitchen sink!"

Daddy grimaced and shook his head. "I think we'd better go back for it. But let's go in Vera and

Ed's car and let everybody else wait for us up there by the filling station. No sense in all of us wasting gasoline."

Although we had each used the outhouse before we left, we kids couldn't pass up the chance to visit the public restroom at the gas station, with its running water and shiny fixtures. Then the boys started chasing each other around the building. When the station owner came to the window and frowned at us, the mothers ordered everybody back on the buses, and we sat there fidgeting and complaining until the men got back. We were a little bit behind schedule now, but Daddy said we would make good time once we got on this new highway.

Mama's side of the family had planned a Barrett reunion in South Bend. We would all meet in a big park that afternoon, to spend a couple of hours together and say goodbye. This meant we would not put on many miles the first day, but at least we would be on our way, and would get settled into our first campground by suppertime. The plan for the second day was to go around Chicago before dawn, avoiding most of the rush hour traffic.

Most of the Barrett relatives had not seen us since Uncle Homer's funeral several years ago, but were still sorry to have us move so far away. Mama's older sister, Blanche, had raised her since their mother's death when she was only four. Their father, Grandpa Barrett, was a traveling salesman, away most of the time until he died in a train accident before Mama's fourteenth birthday.

I barely remembered the Barrett cousins, and none of them were my age; so when we got to the park, I mainly hung around with Betsey and Tucker while Mama talked to Aunt Blanche and Uncle Floyd about old times. When it was time to leave, Mama was the last to get on the bus, and we could see that she was struggling to hold back tears for our sake. I realized she was afraid she might never see her sister again.

Around four o'clock in the afternoon, we found the lakeside campground we were looking for. It would take three campsites to set up the tents, and a fourth one for the vehicles and Aunt Molly's trailer. There were public restrooms and showers down the road, and we could buy wood from the campground office.

Everybody had a job to do. Mine, that first night, was putting oilcloth on two of the picnic tables and setting the table for our own family.

After building the fires and setting up the big tents, the men were ready to just eat and relax. The boys carried water from the pump and put it over the fire to heat. The ladies cooked and served our evening meal, which consisted of fried Spam, fried potatoes, and roasted corn on the cob. There was lemonade for the children and coffee for the grown-ups.

The older girls used metal dishpans for washing the dishes, and poured hot water over them in the same drain racks we used at home. After supper, Uncle Tommy was the first to bring out his musical instruments, and all the other grown-ups did the same. Before the dishes had even been repacked, they had tuned up and lit into the first old favorite, "She'll be Coming 'Round the Mountain," singing in four-part harmony as they played. Some of the other campers drew up folding chairs, smiling and tapping their feet.

Later, as we kids came back from the restrooms all ready for bed, they were still at it. They had gone to quieter melodies now, songs of thanksgiving and prayer. I snuggled into my sleeping bag that night, wondering why I ever felt uneasy about leaving home at all. I dozed off feeling safe and well cared for. What is home, after all, but a loving family?

CHAPTER 4

The second day of our trip west began before dawn. At four o'clock in the morning, my Mama pulled the blanket away from my face and began to give my shoulders a shake.

"Rise and shine, Rosemary. Come on girls, it's time to leave, now!"

I opened my eyes part way and groaned. "It's still night time!"

But there was light from a lamp burning somewhere in the big tent, and people were starting to stir and say "Good morning!"

"Why so early, Mama?" I sat up and reached for the clothes we had set out the night before.

"We have to get an early start, Honey, so we can get past Chicago before the rush-hour traffic begins. Hurry now, so they can take the tents down."

"What about breakfast?" my sister Janet wailed.

"That'll have to wait a few hours this time. Once we are well past the Chicago area, we'll find a park and have something to eat."

"Hurry up, now," Aunt Lou called out. "They're ready to load up!"

"Wait! I have to find my other shoe!"

"Here it is." Mama handed it to me. "Now finish dressing and bring your pajamas and pillow out when you come. Put your things on a picnic table and head for the restrooms. And try to be a little quieter. Other campers are still trying to sleep."

But, with all the shushing and stifling our giggles behind our hands, we still must have caused a major commotion in that campground before we rolled out of there with our crazy caravan. People had come out of their tents and trailers to stare at us.

Now, as planned, we followed the highway toward the Windy City, but instead of going through the main part of the city, we followed the signs directing us south and west of Chicago. By six o'clock, even this bypass highway began to fill up with more cars and trucks and buses than I had ever seen in one place. I cringed as some of them came so close, trying to pass our buses and compete with each other for every inch of space – like a cattle stampede with motors and wheels.

Daddy was just as frightened as we were – I could tell by the sweat on his forehead and by the way he gripped the wheel. But he was doing a good job, and before long the traffic began to thin out a little and he started to relax. Now, most of the cars were coming toward the city, on the other part of the divided highway.

The sun had come out, and we began to play a game counting how many cars of our chosen color we could spot along the highway. I chose yellow. I soon discovered there were not many yellow cars to count, but I was not sorry I chose them, because they were the prettiest. Yellow was the color of butter and morning sunshine.

Soon we came to a town called Westcott. Uncle Tommy signaled for us to pull over and my Daddy signaled back to the others to do the same. This time, Daddy got off and went to talk to his brother outside. They were looking at a billboard that advertised Aunt Jemima Pancakes with a banner across one corner announcing, "ALL YOU CAN EAT PANCAKES, next exit."

"We're going to buy our breakfast today!" Daddy said, beaming as he got back on the bus. He looked at Mama, who had raised her eyebrows.

"Come on," he said. "We've been up for hours, we're all starving, and everybody's too tired to make a fire and cook. We can splurge this once."

We pulled into the parking lot at Casey's Family Restaurant, where the pancakes offer was repeated on the front window.

"Maybe we'd better go in first and see if they can serve 35 more people," Uncle Tommy suggested. He and Daddy went in.

"Doesn't look too crowded," Daddy called back, motioning for us to enter. Two people came out as we were about to go in, and only a couple of the tables were full. We looked around and saw that five tables had been recently vacated, and a waitress was in the process of clearing them all.

The men talked to the proprietor for a few minutes, and then waved for us all to sit down.

Tables were moved around to make room at the ends, and they brought a booster chair for Lucy Belle. Seven could fit at each table.

"We might have to wait awhile for everybody to get fed," Tommy explained, as the place settings were being arranged. "'Nother words, don't be in too much of a hurry, and we'll all get some."

"Bacon and eggs are extra," Daddy cautioned, "so we're just going to fill up on pancakes. Let us do the ordering."

"Look at all the toppings," Mama said. "Regular maple, blueberry, and even brown sugar, the way some of you eat it at home!"

A waitress with long, red fingernails poured coffee all around for the adults. Her painted smile was much bigger than her own lips, and her penciled eyebrows gave her a startled appearance.

"Any beverages for the kids?"

Mama looked at Daddy, and Daddy looked at Tommy. "How about white milk for all of the youngsters. And please serve the kids first when you bring out the pancakes." Aunt Lou took the spoon away from the baby, who was using it to bang on the table.

They were starting us out with one golden pancake, and two pats of butter on each plate, to add while it was still hot.

Lou helped Lucy Belle get started, and looked at Anna Mae struggling with hers. "Cut up your sister's food for her, Trent, will you please?"

Mama poured a spoonful of her hot coffee over my brown sugar, making the rich puddle of syrup that tasted so good.

Uncle Tommy asked the blessing for all of us, and by the time everybody had prepared one steaming pancake to start the meal, some of the boys had finished theirs and were looking around for more. The waitress came with a platter of seconds to place on the first table. Within minutes, she had served all five tables again; and those big pancakes also soon disappeared.

"This was such a good idea!" Molly said. "I know we can't afford to do this every morning, but we probably would have settled for cold cereal and bread today, instead of making a fire and cooking."

"Well, fill up your tummies now," Daddy warned, "because we'll probably try to wait until suppertime to cook again. We can make some sandwiches for lunch, and get out and stretch a little, but we want to stay on the road as much as we can today." With that, he held up a platter again for a refill.

Once we got on the road again, most of us were quiet and drowsy. Daddy said the driving would be somewhat easier now, except in spots where road repair was going on. The cashier at the restaurant had told him to expect rough roads in some areas because during the war, the government had not been able to spend money to maintain its highway system at all.

"The guy said once you get on Route 66, it'll take you as far west as you want to go – but even that has some areas that've never been improved, or have just been neglected too long."

"Well, let's just be thankful they are working on them now," Mama said. "Think of what your folks went through getting there years ago!"

I curled up in my seat next to the window, and watched the landscape moving by. I tried to imagine our ancestors riding in covered wagons, or even walking, covering this same route that we were whizzing over at forty miles an hour.

Daddy seldom talked about those stories. It was actually my Mama who had told us about all that just the day before our out-of-town relatives began to arrive, back in Michigan. She said Daddy didn't remember much about the trip out West, when he was three years old and Tommy was seven – about 1906, she said – but he did have some unhappy memories of the rugged trip back, when he was nine.

His brother Tommy was 13 by then, and Molly, who had been born in New Mexico, was just a toddler. Daddy didn't know why his parents started back in the fall, with that old relic of a wagon and their fourth child on the way. But he did remember a terrific snowstorm in Texas, and a broken wheel. Grandpa Ted had to walk to the nearest farmhouse to get help.

Strangers had taken them in, and Grandpa and both boys had worked for them in exchange for the use of a poorly heated shed, until the baby was born in early March. Then they had moved on, and the baby – Aunt Vera – nearly died of pneumonia before they reached St. Louis.

I looked at my Daddy now, in the driver's seat, and wondered if he was thinking about the olden days, and how he was headed back to the same old homestead after all these years.

We stopped at a two-pump filling station near

Springfield, and decided to look for a roadside park for a quick, cold lunch. Minutes later, we pulled in and parked, glad to get out and stretch again and look for a public restroom. Flush toilets again, and running water, were still a treat because three out of the four families in our group had always lived without indoor plumbing.

Even after all those pancakes for breakfast, we were hungry again. The slices of cold Spam on bread, with glasses of lemonade, tasted fine.

Just as Uncle Tommy pulled his bus out onto the highway again, and ours approached the park exit, we heard horns honking behind us and someone shouting at us to stop. The beds and equipment nearly blocked the back window from view, but my brother Tim leaned over them to see what was the matter.

"Daddy, stop! The others aren't following us! They're trying to tell us something!"

Daddy slowly backed up and Uncle Tommy pulled off the highway and got out. Aunt Vera was shouting and waving, while her family was climbing out of the station wagon. Uncle Ed was getting tools out.

"We've got a flat tire!" Vera called.

At least they had a spare, but the time saved by eating a cold lunch was spent replacing the tire.

When Daddy got back from helping, he asked Mama for another swig of that lemonade. "Startin' to get real hot!"

Later, a speeding motorist tried to pass our whole convoy, ignoring the 40-miles-per-hour limit the government had imposed to save gasoline. But he couldn't make up his mind, so Daddy dropped back to give him room to fit in.

Again the impatient driver started to go around Uncle Tommy, and thought better of it, pulling back in front of our bus, forcing Daddy to use his brakes to avoid hitting him.

This threw us all forward against the upholstered seat in front of us, and most of us caught ourselves with our arms or hands. But my nine-year-old brother Tory hit his face hard against the seat frame, and let out a howl.

"Look! Tory's bleeding!" someone screamed.

Mama grabbed a dishtowel from the shelf above her and moved quickly across the aisle to Tory, then tried to find the source of the blood he was covering up with both hands. "Find a place to stop, Ted! He may be hurt bad!"

Meanwhile, above the wailing, we heard the warning signal of a railroad crossing, and saw the train rounding the bend toward us. Uncle Tommy slowed his bus as he approached the tracks, but the crazy driver pulled out to pass him. He was trying to beat the train, speeding up instead of slowing down.

The car sped across the tracks an instant before the train reached the crossing, its whistle blowing so loud it hurt our ears. The foolish man had made it, but just in time.

Daddy found a factory parking lot and pulled in. Mama helped Tory out of the bus and found a patch of grass for him to sit down on. The bleeding was not profuse, but was flowing hard enough that he kept spitting it out of his mouth.

"Get help, Ted! Hurry! He's bleeding from his nose and mouth, so it must be a head injury!"

Daddy ran into the factory office to find out how to get to the nearest hospital.

"Lou's girl is a nurse's aide!" young Teddy Cooper was shouting. "Here they come now!"

Aunt Lou and her daughter Virginia ran toward us. The girl bent down and pinched Tory's nose, covering the nostrils with her handkerchief. Then she turned to Molly, who was walking toward them.

"Do you have ice in your trailer?"

"Yes, I do." Molly ran to get some. Moments later, Virginia placed ice behind Tory's neck while compressing his nostrils with her fingers.

"I think it's just a nosebleed," she said. "See, he has a little cut on his lip, too. That's starting to clot, now; and I think we have the nosebleed about under control."

She removed her fingers from his nose, and she was right. The bleeding had stopped, and Tory was grinning at her.

His lip was swollen where it had apparently bumped against his own tooth, leaving a quarter-inch cut that wouldn't require any stitches.

"You might have a big, purple lip for a few days," Virginia said. "But I don't think there was any serious harm done."

Daddy came out, relieved to see that Tory was okay, but still feeling bad to have caused an injury to one of his own children.

"There's a doctor's office about a mile down the road. Maybe we should stop in there and have him checked, just in case."

They did that, and came out ten minutes later with a few instructions from the doctor and big smiles on their faces.

Before we boarded the buses and cars again, my Daddy led us in a prayer of thanks, and asked for continued protection and a safe arrival at our destination.

We knew the Lord could be trusted to get us to New Mexico safely, if that was where He wanted us to go. But we didn't know how long the getting there would take.

We hadn't gone more than twenty miles further when trouble struck again.

* * *

Tommy's bus had slowed a little to make room for a passing car to slip in front of him. Daddy tried to slow down, but our bus almost hit Uncle Tommy's from the rear before Tommy began increasing speed for a small uphill portion of the highway. Something was wrong.

Daddy began shouting and signaling Tommy and Uncle Ed. "I can't stop!" he yelled. He aimed for the patch of dirt along the right side of the road, and the long series of jarring bumps set our heads jerking roughly back and forth, gradually bringing our bus to a halt.

Uncle Tommy and the others pulled off as soon as they could.

"Everybody okay?"

"What is it, Ted?"

"Somethin' wrong with the brakes!"

After talking to Daddy, Tommy went on ahead to the next exit to look for a service station. Daddy told my brother Thomas to watch for traffic while he poked around under the bus, studying the problem.

We all prayed that this part of the route wouldn't be heavily traveled, and that Uncle Tommy would be able to get help.

And help came, of course; but, two hours had gone by before both the loaded bus and its tired, waiting passengers could be transported to the service station. There, we learned that the parts had to be ordered by telephone and wouldn't be delivered until the next morning.

One of the mechanics lived nearby, and, with twilight coming on, he offered the use of his father's barnyard and an unused pasture for setting up our camp overnight.

"Once we get our parts delivery," he said, "we'll have you back on the road in no time."

But the parts didn't come until four o'clock the next afternoon, and they were working on another car by then. They promised to work overtime that night to make sure we could leave first thing the next morning.

So, after spending two extra nights in Illinois, and putting a big dent in our travel fund, our caravan was finally on its way again to the Missouri border.

We were excited to be moving again. Daddy took the lead this time. But a while later, I heard him grumbling, and he pulled over to look at the map. Apparently, some stretches of this highway were not clearly marked, and for an hour or so, we had been going the wrong way. We hadn't even left Illinois.

He started off again, the other vehicles following, but it wasn't long before he pulled off once more. This time he got off the bus so he could talk to Tommy. A farmer came by in his truck and offered to help, but when Daddy asked him the way to Route 66, the man just scratched his head and shrugged.

We continued on and got off at the next exit, where we saw a small roadside stand. The lady there said to go back the way we had come, but that turned out to be bad advice.

Hours later, we finally found a filling station owner who knew where to direct us, and resumed the efforts to move our caravan across the state line to Missouri.

CHAPTER 5

We spent Saturday night and Sunday in a large campground near Springfield, Missouri. This was our first Sunday since we left home, and we were not going to travel on the Sabbath, .so we could sleep a little bit later that day.

Just as we began to hear Mama and the Aunts bustling around and smell breakfast cooking, two young men drove into the campground on loud motor scooters. They didn't seem to be campers, just rowdy drifters looking for excitement. They stopped to light up cigarettes, keeping their sputtering motors running, and finally followed the winding dirt roads into the nearby woods.

Later, the girls finished cleaning up and some of the men and boys arranged tables in a semi-circle for our worship service. Daddy and Uncle Tommy went to get their Bibles from their roomy bus compartments, where they both kept them close to their maps and money bags, within reach of their steering wheels. All four families began to gather, and soon our Sunday morning service got under way.

In the middle of Daddy's prayer, the droning vehicles returned, and the smaller children began to stir. They had never seen these motorized bikes before, and couldn't help ooh-ing and ah-ing as they whizzed by. Enjoying the attention, the riders looped around and passed by again, shouting, "Praise the Lord!" and "Hallelujah!"

My cousin Trace motioned for the kids to sit down and keep quiet, and then positioned himself next to the dirt road, so that the next time the revelers came around he was there to try to signal them to pass by quietly, because a prayer was being offered. Instead they made another loop around and shouted bad words at Trace as they passed.

Daddy closed his prayer "in Jesus' name," and said, "Just ignore them; they'll go away."

Uncle Tommy added, "'Nother words, just pretend we don't hear them, and they'll get tired of pestering us."

And it seemed as if they did, after they saw no response to one last loop around, and we were all singing a lively chorus.

Later, after our noon meal, we all took naps – even the grown-ups.

Many of the other campers had gone, and no one stirred as our whole group enjoyed this extra slumber – except my sixteen-year-old brother,

Teddy Cooper, who had crept out to go to the restroom. I woke up hearing a sound outdoors, and, when I opened the window flap next to my bed, I expected to see a raccoon or skunk poking around our campsite looking for a snack. But it was my brother, trying not to wake anybody up and bumping into a water pail on the way out.

I knew better than to get up and disturb everybody, so I just lay there gazing through the screened window. I saw Teddy Cooper, on his way back, come to an abrupt stop and turn toward the parked vehicles as though he was about to run off in that direction.

"Hey!" he shouted. Following his gaze, I saw two motor scooters parked next to Uncle Tommy's bus, with its door ajar. One rider was missing, and I realized the boy was on the bus.

"Hey!" Teddy Cooper shouted again, in his deepest, harshest voice. "Get out of there!"

He began to run toward the bus, but, uncertain what he could do by himself against two older boys, he decided the tents were closer to where he was and changed directions.

"Daddy! Uncle Tommy!" he called. He was gasping so hard that, when Uncle Tommy ran out of his tent, my brother could hardly talk. So he turned and pointed to the bus, just as the missing rider ran out with something in his hand. Then, both of the older boys revved up their bikes. I ran out of the tent.

By the time Uncle Tommy made his way to his bus, with my Daddy and Teddy Cooper close behind, the culprits were disappearing down the highway toward Springfield."

"How did they get in?" Daddy asked, and Uncle Tommy ran up the steps and lifted the compartment lid. The map was still there, and the black leather pouch lay on top of it. But, when he unzipped the pouch, he found it empty.

"Oh, no!" Tommy hid his face with both hands, and appeared to be sobbing as he finally got off the bus and closed the door.

"I could kick myself! I must have left the door ajar when I came to get my Bible," he said.

"I don't know what we're gonna do. Every penny we had was in that pouch."

***

My Daddy called a meeting for the grown-ups while the rest of us gathered up some of our things for re-packing.

I brought out my journal and sketchbook and settled myself behind a big oak tree, just close enough to the urgent meeting to hear some of it, but far enough to keep out of trouble with Mama.

Uncle Howard led the meeting because he had

been an accountant for twenty years. They all agreed that, whatever the cost of Uncle Tommy's gasoline for the remainder of the trip would be, the other three families would share it.

Uncle Howard figured out how much gas Tommy had used up till now, and how far the gas in his tank would take him. By the time he would run out of gas, Howard calculated, we would be crossing the border from Missouri to Oklahoma. We were still almost 800 miles from our destination, four days after we left Michigan. We had covered less than half of our route, and money was going too fast. Daddy never liked to drive more than five or six hours a day. We had of course rested today, on the Sabbath, and had missed nearly two whole days when our bus broke down, and half of another one getting lost.

"But we still had to eat on those days – probably ate more than we did while we traveled," Uncle Tommy commented. "Our food boxes are starting to look skimpy."

"We've still got quite a lot left," Mama said. "We'll all just share what we have."

"Okay," Uncle Howard said, holding his hand up and getting back to the notes he had in front of him. "We'll deal with the gasoline costs first. Our vehicles will need about 100 more gallons of gas apiece, at the current rate of 18 cents per gallon. That's $18 each.

"This trip is taking longer than we thought, so we may not be able to eat as well as we have. We'll try to stretch it out, but we'll probably need to spend at least $3 each at the grocery store before we get to New Mexico."

"Yes, and we're going to need more canned milk for the baby," Lou said emphatically.

"There'll be campground fees for another few nights, unless we can find a free place to stay," Howard reminded them. "That could add up to another $15 for each family."

My Daddy said he was willing to try to spend more hours driving each day. "This might cut that down to two more nights of camping."

Uncle Tommy shook his head in remorse. "I'll keep a good record of anything I have to borrow, and pay it back as soon as possible."

"We're not worried about that," Aunt Molly assured him. "We know you're good for it, and we know you'd have helped us the same way if it had happened to us."

Howard made notes on the lined tablet he had produced from his brief case. "Let's each put twelve dollars into an envelope for Tommy now, and then we'll need to get serious about saving as much as we can for emergencies. We'll have another family meeting in Tulsa."

While they closed their meeting in prayer, I left my listening post and hurried over to the playground, where a ball game was going on.

***

When I walked into the tent later to put my books away, Mama and Daddy were having their own meeting, and counting out money from their own zippered pouch. I stood in silence, so they wouldn't notice me there.

"We only have $65 left, after chipping in for Tommy," Dad said, scrunching his face up like he did when he was worried. "Setting aside the $36 we know we'll probably spend, that only leaves $29 for unknown costs."

Mama put her hand on his arm and spoke gently. "Remember, Margaret still has a nest egg of about $280, from when she worked at the defense plant. She offered to help with the costs of this trip, if we need it."

Daddy brushed away a tear with his big hand. "I don't like letting her do that, Matilda. She worked hard to earn it, and might never have another chance like that again, now that the war's over. If she and Derron get married, they'll need that money."

"Look," Mama answered. "We're all depending

on that inheritance coming through when we get there. If it doesn't – if we misunderstood or it turns out wrong – we'll all be scurrying to get whatever work we can just to survive. But, if it does, and it's waiting for us like the letter said, we can pay her back with interest. We just have to get through these next few days!"

Daddy nodded, seeing that her optimistic view made sense, and agreed that Mama could talk to Margaret about a loan.

***

The night we crossed the border into Oklahoma, it was only 73 degrees – unusually cool for the area in August – so we were unprepared for the day ahead, which reached 73 degrees by six o'clock in the morning, and then climbed about five degrees each hour until high noon. We took turns reading the thermometer attached to the bus near the outside mirrors, and reporting the news.

We looked for a place to stop for lunch and seek shelter from the 103-degree temperature that most of us had never experienced. The local park, near Tulsa, offered no trees for shade, only concrete roofs over concrete tables and benches.

From a store across the street from the park, we bought cold soda pop, and drank it slowly to soothe our dry mouths and blistered lips. Spam sandwiches, with no condiments and dry bread, satisfied our diminished appetites, but the shade did little to cool us.

"We need to stop in town to buy ice," Aunt Molly announced.

"We should save all of these soda bottles and put water in them, for traveling, Mama added. "We don't want to get dehydrated."

"We need to get something for sunburn, too," Aunt Lou remarked. "The tube I brought is almost gone. We need medicated cream and suntan lotion. And Virginia said we should wear long sleeves for sun protection, instead of these short-sleeved shirts."

I didn't bring anything long-sleeved, so Mama said I would have to wear a pajama top.

"Is it going to be this hot in New Mexico?" I asked Mama.

Uncle Tommy heard my question, and said, "Where we'll be, it's a real dry climate. A lot more comfortable, but you have to be more careful of sunburn, because you might not realize how hot it is. 'Nother words, it feels good on your skin but it can still leave you burned and blistered."

My brother Timmy asked, "Is that why cowboys wear those ten-gallon hats a lot?"

Tommy grinned. "I 'spect it is. I recollect a lot of people wore them, cowboys or not."

"It's a good thing I have my old straw hat, at

least," Daddy said. "We'll have to get ourselves some of them hats, once our money comes in."

"Can I get some of those fancy leather boots, too, Daddy?" Teddy Cooper inquired.

"Hold on now," Mama cautioned. "Let's don't go spending money before we get it. Who knows? We might have a lot of expenses to pay with that windfall."

"And we'd better save money to go back with," Daddy said, "in case it doesn't work out."

We stopped in town, and Molly and Howard bought a block of ice for their icebox, and a small bag of chipped ice for the kids to suck on or put in Kool-Aid. The others bought crushed ice, too, for their small coolers. Then we stopped for gas across the street from the ice company.

In the filling station, we saw two American Indians buying tires for a pickup truck. We tried not to stare, because we knew it wasn't polite. But, as we drove out of the station, Timmy said, "Those Indians were dressed just like we are, and they spoke plain old English!"

"You'll see a lot of them from now on. Oklahoma used to be called 'Indian Country,'" Daddy said.

We saw several more Indians while we looked for a park in which to eat our lunch, and where the adults planned to hold another meeting. There was an outdoor market and booths, where people in traditional Indian costumes sold colorful rugs and turquoise jewelry. They were working on baskets and blankets, and the market smelled like straw and old wool.

Later, as we kids sat around concrete tables waiting for our parents' meeting to end, Trace told us this area had been home to Navajo, Apache and Pueblo Indians, decades before our ancestors came through here.

"We'll see Spanish-speaking people too, who came here from Mexico. Many of them are kind of a mixture of Spanish and Indian descent."

As we continued on Route 66, the road led us around and between big mountains. Instead of the green we saw in the Midwest, we were surrounded by orange and purple, and shades of brown – even yellow and pink desert flowers – with the vast blue sky as a sort of backdrop.

The beauty of it all nearly took our breath away. I wished I could sit and paint a picture of it all right now. Even the ground beneath us resembled orange clay instead of the dark brown soil we were used to in Michigan.

But it became harder to enjoy the scenery as we traveled past it and through it, because of the sweltering sunshine. Heat waves shimmered on the distant highways, making us see pools of water where there was no water.

Even sipping on bottled water, and sucking on ice chips, and dipping cold water from the ice chest, couldn't cool us down enough. By the time we pulled into a campground at dusk, Mama was feeling really sick, with nausea, dizzy spells, and a severe headache. Virginia said it could be heat exhaustion.

As soon as the tents were up, Aunt Molly brought out a little pan of ice water from her trailer and poured some into a cup for Mama to drink. Then she dipped a clean dishcloth in water, wrung it out a little, and placed it on Mama's forehead. Soon she dropped off to sleep, and we thought she would be okay.

We ate a cold supper of more Spam and bread and a tiny portion of canned fruit, and went to bed early because the tent was cooler than the outdoors.

After breakfast the next day, we realized it would be hotter that day than the day before. It was already 90 degrees at 9:15 in the morning. When we stopped at a restroom again a couple of hours later, it had climbed to 105 degrees.

We all wore light clothing, with long sleeves. We put on suntan lotion and filled our water bottles. Daddy borrowed Margaret's sunglasses and put on his old straw fishing hat.

Still, we all suffered in the sweltering heat, especially Mama. Several of us developed blistered and peeling lips like she did. Virginia and Aunt Lou came around during another restroom stop and put soothing salve on our lips. I felt immediate relief.

By noon, nausea came over Mama once again, and her head ached worse than it had the day before. Aunt Lou and Virginia hovered over her, changing the cold cloth on her forehead as often as they could. Virginia rode on our bus, so she could take care of her. She spoke to Daddy in whispered tones, and they soon told us to wait on our buses while they took Mama to a local clinic with Ed and Vera's station wagon.

They were gone a long time, so Aunt Molly said we should get out and fix something to eat; and then Aunt Lou and Vera came back to tell us they had taken Mama to the hospital, because of severe dehydration. Daddy would not leave her side, so they came back without him. Uncle Tommy and Trace began to set up the tents in the same park where we had eaten lunch.

Then, Uncle Howard went to the hospital with Tommy, carrying his leather pouch with him to pay some money on the hospital bill.

"May I go along?" It was my sister Margaret,

her voice barely heard across the banter and commotion, just as they headed for the station wagon. "I need to talk to my Daddy." They nodded, and she climbed in, carrying her purse.

Hours passed, and Aunt Molly rounded up some of my older cousins to help get the evening meal started. We ate rice and beans, canned vegetables, and applesauce for dessert.

We all prayed for my Mama, and for wisdom in making our food and gas money last the rest of the trip. We had more than 600 miles to go, and more campground fees to pay. Uncle Howard had already told us that the hospital required payment up front for anyone who didn't live in the county.

Daddy and the others came back before dark, saying that Mama was doing better, but would have to stay in the hospital at least one more day. There was a possibility she could come home tomorrow evening, after the doctor's afternoon rounds. Daddy would go back in the morning to sit with her again.

***

We made Cream of Wheat and campfire biscuits early the next day, before the temperature rose too much. While my Daddy and Uncle Tommy were gone that morning, my cousin Trent started a game of "Capture the Flag." Soon we were all involved in group games, except the Aunts and two of the

Uncles, who just rested in the tents and sipped ice tea.

At noon we had very small portions of canned beef stew, and peanut butter sandwiches, with water from our own bottles. Afterwards, some of the youngsters grumbled that they were still hungry. But they knew enough not to say it in front of the Aunts, because they were doing the best they could.

Aunt Lou had pretended not to have any appetite because of the heat, and the other ladies served themselves half as much as they gave each child.

An hour before it was time to start supper, Uncle Tommy drove in, and both Daddy and Mama were with him.

We squealed and ran and surrounded her as she got out of the station wagon, all determined to get our hugs first.

She giggled, and Daddy said, "Take it easy! Give her a chance to relax, now, so she won't have to go right back there!"

Mama still looked a little peaked, but full of smiles and glad to be back.

Daddy was full of smiles, too, and so was Uncle Tommy. They looked at each other and grinned like boys raiding a cookie jar, then went back to the car and returned with some packages.

"Groceries!" I squealed, jumping up and down, and the Aunts began to unload them at the nearest picnic table. Aunt Vera had tears in her eyes, and Aunt Molly turned and looked at Howard, who looked thoughtful.

They had brought bread and milk and margarine, link sausages, frozen meatballs, and a large canned ham. There was also a big sack of potatoes and other fresh vegetables.

When we saw Uncle Tommy taking three 12-packs of Coca Cola and two bags of chipped ice out of the car, we couldn't believe it.

All of the Aunts were now in tears.

"We're not going to go hungry, Lou," Tommy said, holding back tears himself, now. "In fact, when we get to Tucumcari, we're going to eat breakfast out again!"

"But, how?" Aunt Vera gasped.

Uncle Howard was the first to guess their secret. "So you did call him, right? I told you he'd help, now that we're close to Chaparral."

Lou followed Howard's gaze to Uncle Tommy, and exclaimed, "What did you do?"

"I called Horton, the lawyer – told him where we were and what was happening, and he called Todd Alverson, our cousin. He's the one that's administering Grandma's estate, and could release some of the money on his own say-so. He wired me a thousand dollars against what we'll have coming, and both Ted and I talked to him on the phone for a while. He's really a nice guy!"

Supper that night was one of the best meals we'd had since we left Michigan. Aunt Lou and Virginia cooked the ham, with potatoes and gravy, corn-on-the-cob, and fresh green beans. Aunt Molly made some cabbage slaw, and Aunt Vera served up strawberry shortcake for dessert.

The night was still warm until after midnight, but we sipped our cold soda pop and used colorful paper fans we had made while waiting for our parents to come home that day.

We left the park at six o'clock the next morning, stopped to have a roadside breakfast, and then drove until 11 o'clock at night. Daddy said Cousin Todd suggested resting from mid-morning till dusk, and then driving at night. We drove for another two hours that evening, and then pulled into a campground in Shamrock, Texas, because Daddy was getting sleepy.

They roused us at 3:30 the next morning. the day we left Texas and crossed over into New Mexico. It was 10:30 by the time we drove into Tucumcari, but we ate store-bought muffins and bananas to hold us over. Then, as promised, we all went into the Hueve con Carne Restaurant and enjoyed their breakfast specials – this time with eggs and bacon and

American fries, whatever we wanted, washed down with orange juice and cocoa.

The men lingered over coffee refills and studied their directions to Chaparral. Tommy asked Uncle Howard to divide up what was left of the loan proceeds between the four families, giving them each more than two hundred and twenty five dollars to use and have deducted from their promised inheritance.

Daddy paid back Uncle Howard and Margaret for Mama's medical bill, and put gas and oil in the bus at the next filling station. We rented motel cabins just outside Albuquerque, so we could have a good night's rest and a chance to spruce up before we showed up at the attorney's office in Chaparral.

"We may have made this trip on a shoe string," Daddy said, "but we don't have to go there looking like a bunch of street urchins."

***

It was going to be our last night on the road, and it was a special treat to be allowed to have a shower before our outdoor church service, and cool off with electric fans all afternoon and overnight. Each little adobe cabin had a clothesline out back, so we could each wash out one of our best sports outfits to wear for our arrival the next day. Mama shampooed my hair and did it up in braids, and the older girls curled their hair, rolling it up on bit of rags the way they had back home.

Daddy brought in a rollaway cot for me, and my Mama and three sisters slept in the two double beds provided with the cabin.

Aunt Molly, in their nearby cabin, heated up our meatballs in her big electric pot, mixing in the spaghetti and left-over green beans. We went down and filled our paper plates and brought them back to eat in our own cabins. Then we climbed into our pajamas and went to bed early.

On Monday, the last day of traveling, we vacated our seven cabins at the motel and departed just before dawn. Coming down around the winding road into Albuquerque, the few lights already on looked like stars dipping down among the mountains – a magical view I would always remember. Without stopping to eat breakfast, we covered the last 200 miles into Chaparral.

We drove slowly through the quaint little town. The traditional Spanish architecture – even of the bank and county building – suited the climate. The mountains in the background made the town look even tinier by comparison.

Daddy said it was hard to find traces of anything he remembered, but we saw a public school he thought might be on the site of the two-room schoolhouse established by Alverson uncles back in 1906.

Daddy, as a nine-year-old, and his brother Tommy, at 13, had been taken out of school when Grandpa Ted and Grandma Ellen abruptly sold their 160-acre homestead to Uncle Thomas and headed back east, in spite of Grandpa Thurmond's objections.

Mama had told us, the night we stayed in the cabins, about that trip long ago. Unlike ours, it had not been well-planned, and had been nearly disastrous for Daddy's family. Uncle Tommy remembered more about those early days out West, but Daddy remembered that horrible trip east. Daddy told Mama he never dreamed he'd be making the long trip back to Chaparral.

Not wanting us to arrive hungry at Attorney Horton's office, Uncle Tommy recommended stopping at a county park to eat and regroup before driving downtown.

After awhile, another group arrived at the park. Some of the young children wandered our way a few times, watched us for awhile, and then ran giggling back to their own tables. Then older children began to come around, loitering quite close to us but not saying a word. We had grown used to people staring at us, being a large group with our converted buses and old cars; but these onlookers seemed different, somehow.

While we ate, some of them whispered nearby, and a few of the braver ones snuck around to peek into the windows of our buses – disheveled as they were by now, and coated with dust and sand on the outside.

Two girls near my age finally walked over to watch us at a closer range. I smiled at them, and said "Hi!" One of them nodded.

The other girl, who was dressed in a white denim pant suit, spotless saddle shoes, and bobby sox, gawked at my dusty sandaled feet. She turned her back, tossed her wavy red hair, and started to walk away. Then she turned again and asked, "Do you people live in these buses?"

"Oh, no!" I said. "I mean, we don't live anywhere right now, but we slept in tents all the way here. Except last night, when we slept in cabins, with real plumbing and everything."

Her response was a smug expression, but the first girl gave me a half-smile and spoke.

"My name's Ginny Alverson, and this is my cousin Carol."

"Alverson!" I cried. "That's my last name, too. I'm Rosemary Alverson, and we came here from Michigan. Maybe we're cousins!"

Before she could answer, her companion led her away. "C'mon, Ginny. We have to get back!"

As they both walked away, I heard her remark, "My Mama says they're just here to try to get Grandma's house."

I didn't say anything about our visitors until we were back on the bus. Then I asked Mama about it. "What did that girl mean?"

Mama measured her words before answering. "Those people must be some of our relatives."

Margaret overheard the conversation and said, "You mean they knew who we were and never came to greet us?"

Mama sighed. "Well, they may feel a bit wary of us. For whatever reason, Grandma Elizabeth apparently left almost everything to Grandpa Ted's branch of the family, and most of them don't even remember us."

"Trace says that half of the people in this town are Alversons, and probably many more are related by marriage," Margaret said.

"He's probably right. Grandpa Thurmond had a big family, and most of them must have stayed near the old homestead."

"Judging by the nice ranches and fine houses around here," Margaret said, "they must have done very well for themselves over the years."

It was a short trip to the business section of town. We parked all four vehicles in the bank parking lot, and we kids waited with Mama and Aunt Lou, while Daddy, Uncle Tommy, Aunt Vera, and Aunt Molly kept their appointment with Mr. Horton at his law offices.

Twenty minutes after they went in, they came out with two other men. A gray-haired man in a white suit, who was obviously Attorney Horton, locked the door behind them and walked in the opposite direction from the parking lot.

The younger man, who was tanned and sturdy-looking, walked with our group toward the parking lot, as jovial and amicable as if he'd known them forever. They headed directly toward us in our parked vehicles, and he was already reaching out his hand as he boarded our bus, greeting my Mama first and then making the rounds to introduce himself to all of us.

"Hi there, cousin!" he said to Mama, squeezing her hand and then greeting my brothers and sisters. "I'm Todd Alverson! Howdy! Good to finally meet you folks. Bet you're real tired from all that traveling!"

He even smiled right at me, as if he knew me; then, working his way back to my Mama, he said, "I was asking Ted if you could all follow me over to

Alverson Drive, where the houses are. Maybe we could meet tomorrow morning and take a little tour of the properties."

"Sounds good to me!" Mama answered, and Todd backed out of the bus smiling broadly, then went over to greet the rest of our group.

For the first time, I felt like we had found a member of our family here in New Mexico. He seemed truly glad we came.

Todd even looked a little bit like my Daddy, in a way. He walked like him, and looked like a younger, livelier, more muscular version of my Daddy, with the intense brown eyes even more intense, and the full bottom lip even fuller than Daddy's. He was taller than Daddy, yet shorter than Uncle Tommy, with a thicker chest and firmer jaw, but his thick and wavy hair made his receding hairline seem more youthful. His jaw line actually looked more like my cousin Trace and Aunt Molly, and he had the same dimpled cheeks as Molly and my sister Janet.

But it was not merely the slight physical resemblance that spoke to my heart. It was his obvious and sincere feelings about our arrival – more than just a polite welcome.

Daddy got in and smiled at Mama. Then he whipped out something from his shirt pocket and unfolded it. Mama leaned forward to see what it was, and I looked over her shoulder. It was a check, made out for Twenty-Four Thousand, Seven Hundred and Fifty Dollars!

Her jaw dropped as her eyes widened. "Already?" she asked, and Daddy grinned. "All we had to do was sign two papers, and they handed us the checks! 'Course, we have to put money into the business, ya' know, out of this."

He revved up the motor and backed up, following Tommy out of the lot. "We'll come back and open a bank account tomorrow. Right now, Todd's going to show us our houses and give us the keys!"

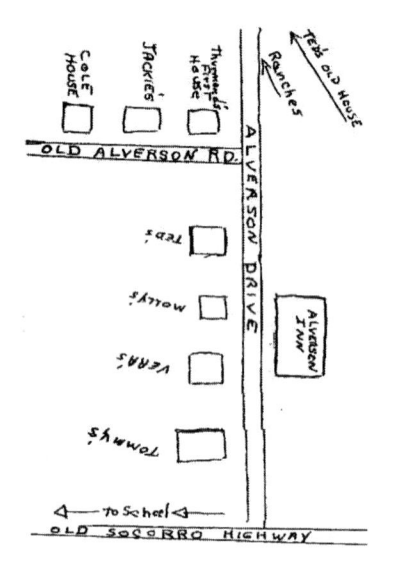

by Rosemary A., 1946

CHAPTER 6

Alverson Drive, a long, paved road, ran from the north end of Main Street all the way to the Old Socorro Highway.

"All this land used to be part of our holdings," Daddy told us on the way to our destination. "These ranches used to be 160 acres each. Todd says grazing land got scarce because of the mesquite that crowds out everything else out here; takes all the water. They'd try to get rid of it, and it would just grow back. Pretty soon most of the land wasn't worth anything except to build on, so they sold it, all but 60 acres apiece closest to the creek. Some lots are smaller than that. Since there's no open range anymore, they mainly keep their best cattle for other ranchers to get a start with, you know. The next generation mostly makes a living some other way."

Then we passed a number of stately homes with huge, well-tended yards and luscious gardens, watered by irrigation systems. We could see horse stables here and there, and rows of cottonwood trees or adobe walls between the homes, for privacy.

About a half mile before Alverson Drive intersected with the highway, we saw a street sign that read "Old Alverson Road," marking a dirt road leading off of the paved drive. It was lined with poorly constructed older homes in different states of disrepair. Children played on a tire swing in one yard, and housewives hung their laundry in cluttered back yards.

As the road came closer, I expected we would be turning off here. Maybe one of these would be our house. But Cousin Todd drove on without turning, and pointed to an enormous house on his left, a three-story Spanish hacienda with boarded-up shutters and a lettered sign spelling out ALVERSON INN.

Todd signaled and came to a stop. Daddy and Uncle Tommy got out to talk with him. We couldn't hear what they said, but Todd pointed first to the big building, then to the opposite side of the street, where four substantial, freshly-painted two-story houses faced the inn.

Daddy finally came back and announced, "We're here!"

He pulled the bus into the paved driveway of one of the houses, Number One Alverson Drive, while Uncle Howard and Aunt Molly were driving into Number Two, a slightly smaller version of the same house. Uncle Ed and Aunt Vera were directed to Number Three, and the very biggest house on the end, Number Four, had been assigned to Uncle Tommy's family.

We all got out, and I ran to give Betsey a hug. "We'll be next-door neighbors!" I squealed.

Todd was talking to Daddy again. "This was Grandpa Thurmond's second house," he said. "The first one, not counting the little dugouts they stayed in while they built their homes, still stands over here on what we now call Old Alverson Road. That was in 1906. As they prospered, Grandpa had a better house built for them here, somewhere around 1916; then some of the other family members built on these two-acre lots he gave them."

Tommy gazed at the dilapidated house across the road we had passed. "I think I remember Grandma and Grandpa living over there, but I don't remember the other ones. Seems like we lived over that way from them." He pointed toward one of the nice homes we had passed.

"Those houses were torn down a long time back," Todd answered.

"All the ranch land included just about everything you saw from here to town. 'Course there wasn't much of a town back then – a trading post, probably a livery stable and a few tradesmen setting up.

"Each one of the grown-up sons and married daughters had their own section of land, but Grandpa's idea was for everybody to work together and split the income. He called himself "just an old socialist farmer" in those days. Used to read a lot of John Ruskin books, and that's where he got this idea of all of them moving here together, with their spouses and kids and all. Never did get over that, even when some of the sons moved away, or threatened to move if they couldn't go it on their own."

He pointed again at the inn across the road. "He built this 22-room house in the early twenties, urging his grown-up grandchildren to move in with him.

Only a few of them gave it a try, some moving back out and others moving in, thinking they were going to save some money.

"After he died in 1929, Grandma got tired of seeing all those empty bedrooms, and started taking in boarders outside the family. She didn't need the money, of course; just got lonely, because most of her kids kind of made themselves scarce.

"She owned a working ranch and a stack of land contracts for income, and I guess she made some good investments around the state. Didn't even lose much during the Depression.

"Grandma had more business sense than Grandpa had, and she turned every dollar over more times than a tumbleweed in a wind storm!"

"Sounds like quite a lady," Daddy remarked.

"Well, here are your keys. Get yourselves some rest, and I'll stop in tomorrow – say around ten? We'll walk over and tour the inn. Feel free to bring the kids. Then you and Tommy and I will take a ride around while I explain some of the holdings being distributed right now."

Cousin Todd turned to leave, and we turned to walk up the long cement path to the front door.

"By the way, Matilda," he added as an afterthought, and Mama turned around. "My parents were the last ones to live in this house. They did some updating over the years, while they owned it, and then Elizabeth bought it back from my Pop, after my Mom died, to keep it in the family, you know. My father lives in town, now, in a small apartment.

"We left their old furniture in there, but feel free

to replace anything here if you want to." Again, he said goodbye and left.

We stepped into a fully furnished home, a little bigger than the one we'd rented back in Michigan, but this one was ours to keep.

Todd's mother, Sarah Alverson, had certainly been a real homemaker.

It was tastefully decorated and brightened up with lovely, handcrafted heirlooms; yet they had added a lot of modern décor and conveniences.

Wooden Venetian blinds at the living room windows were color-coordinated with floral chintz draperies, and the couch and one chair were covered with the same cream, green, and orange material. Parquet flooring extended into the formal dining room, with plain beige area rugs in each room that was visible from the front entrance. A piano and a roll top desk fit easily in the large living room, as well.

A winding staircase led to the second floor, but two bedrooms were on the main floor.

The master bedroom, off the living room, had a white enameled bureau, chest of drawers and dressing table, all with brass handles and mirrored frames. The bed was covered first with a sunny yellow antique satin spread, and then a lovely white, hand-crocheted spread in a sunburst pattern, on top.

A real bathroom that you could enter from either the master bedroom or the dining room had a built-in tub, a flush toilet, and a wash basin with little drawers in the built-in cabinet below. There was even a laundry chute and a linen closet with a full-length mirror on the door. The scent of Johnson's Wax, Old Dutch Cleanser, and vinegar lingered from a recent cleaning.

In the dining room there was some pretty furniture that Mama said was called Duncan Phyfe. A dark brown china cabinet still displayed a full set of "Sunday best" dishes, and held an old set of silverware in a velvet-lined drawer.

The drop leaf table would extend to hold ten people, and had lyre-back chairs, with green and black striped upholstery and extra chairs stored in a closet off the hall leading to the kitchen.

Mama ran her hands over the smooth counters and admired the built-in porcelain sink, shiny chrome faucets, big cupboards, and a Magic Chef gas range, just waiting for the home-cooked meals we all missed so much. There was an electric refrigerator, too, with a little freezer that required no ice delivery, just like she had seen in the latest Sears catalogue!

A shiny linoleum floor covering in the kitchen had little black and red diamonds on a white background, and a black border.

She opened up a cupboard and found a flour bin, with a built-in sifter and all. Another held an ironing board that dropped down from its narrow cabinet, while still another contained a hidden wastebasket.

On the other side of the kitchen, we found another hallway. Turning right we saw a pantry, a coat closet, and a door leading to the second bedroom. This one had twin beds in it, a painted chest of drawers, wrought-iron hooks for clothing, and ruffled curtains at the window.

The hallway, turning left, also led to a screened-in back porch.

The three bedrooms upstairs had not been used in many years, but somebody had come in to sweep and dust very recently. There were fresh flowers in every bedroom. The wallpaper was a bit faded, but there were homemade rag rugs on the floor, new-looking window shades, and clean curtains that smelled like Ivory Snow. Someone, besides the late Aunt Sarah, cared about making these rooms say "Welcome!"

The double beds had rounded metal frames, good springs, and clean mattresses. Each had a big oak dresser with a mirror, and only a few chips and scratches as evidence of twenty years of raising children here, long ago.

One room had a sturdy library table, with some old yellowed volumes of hard-cover classics still on its shelves. On the wall, there was an old photograph of Great-grandpa Thurmond's family, probably taken just a few years before they came to New Mexico.

One room contained a maple rocking chair that squeaked when you moved it, so old and delicate that Mama guessed it could have been brought from Missouri in the Alverson wagons, back in 1906. How many infants, we wondered, had been cuddled and rocked to sleep in it?

These beds still had faded home-sewn quilts on top of real linen sheets and pillowcases. In the corner of the second room stood the old treadle sewing machine on which some of the bedding and curtains were probably made, and cedar chests at the foot of both beds.

Mama wiped away the tears in her eyes and began to assign the bedrooms.

For now, Margaret and I would share the one with twin beds, downstairs. There was room there for Margaret's vanity dresser, which they had taken apart and squeezed into the back of the bus. It would look nice with the white floor tile with golden flecks, and the white painted dresser.

I wished I could have the room to myself after Margaret got married next summer, but in a family as big as ours, that wasn't possible. One of my other sisters would move in.

Daddy and Teddy Cooper were examining the basement, with its Maytag wringer washing machine and coal-burning furnace. I crept down the narrow stairs to take a look.

A dank odor permeated the basement, but there was no sign of lingering water or mold. Two big galvanized tubs still stood by the old washing machine, and there were quite a few old tools still hung on pegs.

Canning jars and a couple of large pots still filled the wooden shelves, along with some outdated kitchen equipment, like ancient meat grinders, scales and butter crocks. There were also old flat irons and rug beaters on a set of shelves so weak it was about ready to fall apart.

The old storm door, too, had seen its best days, and would probably have to be replaced. This house was built like the one Grandpa Thurmond had left back in Missouri, it was clear. They didn't realize that New Mexico did not have the kind of storms they had in the Midwest, Daddy said. "Remember, winters don't get much below fifty degrees, as a rule. We'll get the coal bin filled up in October, and it might last us a whole season, maybe two."

By and large, he said as he looked around, the house was in good repair. He told Mama that a home like this, with no rent to pay, had been worth uprooting ourselves for – or, at least it would be, if the family business turned a profit to live on before long. He reminded her that the cash inheritance would not last long, unless they could get money coming in on a regular basis.

Then he remembered he had to start unloading the bus. He set the boys to carrying things in and told them to get the nod from their mother on each item, whether to continue on down the basement with it, or set it down in a room of her choice. The rollaway cots, he knew, would have to go to the cellar for storage.

Each of us girls stood ready to claim our own boxes of clothes and put them away ourselves.

"All of the blankets and sheets and pillowcases can go right down the laundry chute," Mama instructed Margaret and Carrie. "And put the pillows in the upstairs bedrooms." Those they found in the main floor bedrooms were in excellent condition.

Soon she had all the kids, even Tory, saving her steps by taking various items to appropriate rooms, at least. Some of it was just plopped down in front of whatever cupboard or closet Mama wanted them in, to be dealt with later.

She confided in Margaret: "I'm beginning to wonder how we'll have time to keep this place up, once we start working at the hotel."

"Mama, you'll have to learn to delegate more. The younger kids are old enough to do some chores - even Rosemary and Tory. We'll have to start teaching them how you want things done." I wasn't sure I liked the idea of more work, but I knew Margaret was right.

"I'm hungry!" one of the boys complained.

"Yeah, when are we gonna have supper?"

Mama hadn't realized it was getting so late.

Daddy stopped what he was doing and asked, "We're not going to eat Spam again, are we?"

She realized then that we were not close enough to the stores to send one of the kids over.

She looked at Daddy. "If I make a list, would you make a quick trip to the grocery store?"

He chuckled, remembering he would have to drive the bus into town. "Looks like some of that money'll have to be spent on a car. I wonder what they'll give me for a trade-in credit."

By 6:30, Mama and Margaret had cooked up some spaghetti with meat sauce on the new kitchen stove, and Carrie did her best at making a salad. I put one of our oil cloths on the pretty metal table in the kitchen.

"Wash that cloth off real good, Rosie, before you start setting the table," Mama told me. "I'm sure it's dusty from being under the bus."

Janet made a pitcher of Kool-Aid, but there was no ice to put in it yet.

"Fill up those ice cube trays in the freezer, Margaret, so we'll have some for tomorrow."

"Mama, I don't know if we'll all fit around the kitchen table."

"It opens up, Honey," she said. "Timmy, help your sister slide that table open, will you please? The bottom layer just pulls out and joins with the top layer. You'll see."

"Only four chairs, though, Mama. Shall I use the good ones?"

"There are four more of these kitchen chairs in the dining room closet, Tim," Mama said. "You'll have to get those two off the porch to go with them."

When we all sat down at the kitchen table, Daddy said, "Let's sing our blessing tonight, like we used to."

We all joined hands and bowed our heads, and sang:

Be present at our table, Lord.
Be here and everywhere adored.
Thy creatures bless, and grant that we
May feast in Paradise with Thee.

For the first time, Mama told Janet to wash the dishes and me to dry them and put them away. "Tomorrow," she said, "You can wash, Janet, and Rosemary can dry. If we're going to be running a hotel and restaurant over there, it's going to take all of us to keep things in order at home. This is going to be your regular job, now, girls. Along with some other chores, and helping to keep an eye on Tory when I'm not here."

"I don't mind, Mama," I said. "But you were working at another job back in Michigan, too. Why didn't you need me to help then?"

"Two reasons," she said. "This time, all of the older children will have jobs at the inn, too. And, besides, you're not little girls anymore. Eleven and thirteen is plenty big enough to take on some responsibilities at home."

I really didn't mind. Taking care of such a beautiful house would be fun, and having Mama recognize me as growing up – well, that made me feel proud. Little did I know how much I would have to do, once our family business got going.

Margaret got to have the bed next to the window, but I got to choose which two drawers I wanted for my things. I chose the top two, so I wouldn't have to bend down to get my underwear and pajamas.

The white beds looked so nice, with tiny pink roses all over the white cotton coverlets, and big plumped up pillows in their hand-embroidered pillow cases. The first thing Margaret did was ask Thomas to help her put Derron's picture on the wall, and put together her vanity dresser in one corner.

I put my one dress and my flowered housecoat on hangers and hung them on wrought iron hooks, and then put my neatly folded blue jeans and tee-shirts in the dresser. Margaret took a bath before bed, even though we had just taken showers in the motel cabin the night before.

So much had happened, I could hardly believe that, less than two weeks ago, we were still in Michigan. I knew our lives would never be the same again.

When I prayed at bedtime that first night, I thanked the Lord for getting us here safely, and for providing such a pretty house for our family. But, most of all, I prayed that He would help me find more people as nice as Cousin Todd in our new neighborhood, especially when school started up the following week.

***

"We're going to go look at the inn today," Mama said at breakfast, "and then get some groceries. And as soon as we can, we're going to spend a whole day shopping. We have to get you children ready for school."

"Mama," Janet inquired. "Do we have to go school shopping on the bus?"

"Well, it's a long walk to town, dear. I think we should count our blessings, and not grumble about our means of transportation."

Around ten o'clock, there was a knock at the front door. As expected, it was Cousin Todd, ready to take us through the Alverson Inn.

He sat down at the kitchen table to have a cup of coffee with Daddy.

"As you already know, Grandma Elizabeth really wanted that big house to become a hotel again," he said. "I think a venture like this could work. We're expecting a big surge of tourist trade in the Southwest – maybe even a population boom, now that the war is over. Some of this could spill over into small towns like ours, near the new highway they're going to build."

Daddy said, "Aren't there one or two motels already, though, at the edge of town? I'm wondering if our inn will be big enough to make any money at it, ya know?"

Todd reflected on this. "We sort of thought a good hotel restaurant would help. Some of the people around here have a little money to spend, and now that food is more readily available, a good place to dine out might go over real good."

Daddy nodded. "I'm anxious to see what we've got to work with. I spent a few years working in the hospitality trade, as a boy in St. Louis. I enjoyed it, but it's been a long time."

Uncle Tommy knocked on our door, and Mama invited him to come in for coffee.

"Thanks for the invite, Matilda," he said, "but I'd just as soon get on with our tour. 'Nother words, I'm anxious to see the inn."

Daddy and Cousin Todd finished their last gulp and went on out.

"C'mon, kids, if you want to go. Just stick with us, and don't be runnin' around over there. You might as well get used to some ground rules, because we don't want to chase our customers away once we get some."

Mama said "You kids wash your hands and face, and comb your hair before we go. Teddy Cooper, you've worn that shirt for the past two days! Go get a clean one on."

CHAPTER 7

We walked across Alverson Drive to Grandma Elizabeth's old house to meet with Cousin Todd, who had already left by car with Uncle Tommy and my Daddy, to show them some property Grandma Elizabeth had left to other relatives.

They were already circling the building while they talked, inspecting the three story structure made of white adobe with redwood trim. Even with its elaborate tile roofing and fancy details, it reminded me of the simple Spanish-style buildings we had seen downtown. Built in 1925, it was the extraordinary structure that Grandpa Thurmond built to celebrate his success and to hopefully attract his grandchildren, Todd said.

"He still hadn't given up his ideas of large, family groups living and working together and sharing whatever they had," he explained.

"While some of his grandchildren agreed to come and live with them, during the Great Depression, he put them to work growing and selling vegetables for a while. But Grandpa didn't really have a head for business, and most of them didn't stay long. It was Grandma Elizabeth who built up the family treasures with good investments, after he died, during the early thirties. She came through the Depression without much loss at all. She started investing in this town again, and bought some good stocks and bonds. She just liquidated most of those into cash a couple of years ago."

An imposing sign, ALVERSON INN, stood on high posts, and a less professional-looking sign had been nailed underneath it saying CLOSED FOR REMODELING.

Two cars, besides Todd's, sat in the small parking lot – a beat up '38 Ford and a Dodge convertible.

"Tad Alverson's grandson is here, as kind of a live-in caretaker," Todd explained. "I don't know who the Dodge belongs to. He must have company."

A loud radio sang out a lively Dorsey tune and someone yelled, "I think somebody's here!" Todd tried knocking and calling out, "Hey, Robby? Open up there, man!"

Then we heard the lock click, and the door opened. A disheveled-looking young man in a polo shirt and jeans let him in, and slapped his forehead in surprise when Tommy and my Daddy followed him in. The rest of us hung back, as though still inspecting the building exterior.

"Oh, sorry, sir, I clean forgot! Is that today?"

"It sure is, buddy. I told you we'd be here around ten!" Todd turned and motioned for all of us to come in. Robby had obviously not expected us, and began apologizing for being "in a bit of a mess, here."

He introduced his wife, Debbie, a young woman about Margaret's age, who appeared ready to bear a child in the very near future.

Another couple lounged on a long divan, where an ashtray nearly overflowed onto an expensive-looking coffee table. The man wore a wool beret cocked on one side of his head, which I thought was silly to wear indoors on a 90-degree summer day. His stockinged feet rested on the table in front of him.

The blonde lady next to him wore a red skirt with a ruffled hem and a white, Spanish-style blouse that revealed her shoulders. She wore very bright lipstick, and had bare feet. She was painting her toenails and balancing a lit cigarette on the rim of a piece of Navajo pottery.

"These are my friends, Sonny and Delores," Robby said, without introducing us. He looked around, somewhat embarrassed, and began to clear off the three dining room tables. One of them had the remains of their breakfast; a second one still displayed last night's chili supper and several glasses; and the third table had an open bag of potato chips and several pop bottles strewn around, bottle caps, carton and all.

By the odor of Robby's breath, I thought, there was more than soda pop involved; maybe his delay in opening the front door was so he could get rid of the beer bottles.

The visitors got up and prepared to leave, and Robby's wife excused herself and left the room. Todd invited us all to sit down in the big dining room-living room area.

"Robby, I'd like to have a word with you in the kitchen, please?"

Todd closed the door behind them, but their raised voices carried enough for us to catch a few words.

"Just because Grandma's gone, don't think you're going to get away with hanging around and wrecking this place! Have these people been living with you?"

"Not exactly," we heard Robby respond.

Then Todd lowered his voice and talked to him some more.

"Nobody said we couldn't have visitors!"

"... partying in here, smoking up the place ..."

"Maybe we should look for another place to live,

after the baby comes ..."

"... won't be up to me. It'll be up to the new owners, sitting right out there. You're not starting out very well, if you want to ask them any favors. I can tell you right now, they won't allow anybody to booze it up over here."

"We weren't boozing it up. I drank one beer to be sociable, and my friends had a couple."

Todd's voice went lower and calmer, so we knew he was trying to help this young man, not just blow off steam. By the time they came out of the kitchen, he had regained his composure and Robby, still a bit red in the face, began to scurry around and clean up the area.

After Robby disappeared somewhere in the building, Todd mentioned that Grandma Elizabeth had a tendency to take some of her great-grandchildren under her wing, if she saw they were not on the best terms with their own parents. They had a lot of respect for her, and some of them took it hard when she died.

"Sometimes the older folks thought they were just impressed with her money, but, they didn't understand; she really did have a close relationship with some of them, and knew how to bring out the best in them."

Todd must have thought quite a lot of her

himself, judging from the way he talked.

"Some of the great-grandchildren rented rooms from Grandma for awhile, but some were unemployed, and she'd let them stay anyway. Give them a few odd jobs to do, and call them employees."

"Maybe she was just lonely and liked their company," Mama said.

"Could be. She used to tell me I was one of the few of her relatives over thirty who ever came here."

"So, Robby and his wife lived here before she died?"

"Off and on, at least. We thought we'd need somebody to watch the place until you got here, and we'd help those two out at the same time. I didn't expect this! Grandma would never have put up with it, and we shouldn't either."

Tommy and my Daddy nodded in understanding, and then began to look around.

The extra-large living room and dining room had been made into one, about 60 feet long and 30 feet wide. A door at one end led to another good-sized room that held a billiards table.

"This wall could be taken out, too, if you wanted to make it even bigger," Todd suggested. "If you operated a hotel-restaurant, you might get a lot of customers from around town, along with travelers passing through."

He led us into the kitchen and showed us one of the bathrooms leading from it. "There are two other bathrooms, one on each floor."

As they talked, some of us kids wandered away and began to explore. We opened a door to the back hall and discovered a small apartment back there, showing signs that Robby and Debbie probably lived in it.

"We shouldn't be in here," Trace advised. "We'd better wait for someone to invite us in."

We climbed the wide staircase, anxious to explore the upper rooms. There were twelve large bedrooms in all – six bedrooms, plus a bathroom and linen closet, on each upstairs floor. All of the rooms were spacious, clean and simply furnished, but one of them showed evidence of Robby's friends having used it. There were two disheveled sleeping bags on the double bed, cigarettes and a tabletop radio on the dresser, and a guitar propped up in a corner. Two empty beer bottles lay on the hardwood floor.

"I'll see that Robby gets this all cleaned up before Monday," Todd promised.

Eventually, we all got to see most of the rooms, and Todd promised to give us the keys as soon as he got more copies made. More careful inspection could be done after that.

"I thought I'd give you folks a chance to settle in at home, and then some of you might want to start having some meetings over here to decide what you want to do."

We thanked him, and began to make our way out of the building and across the road. Todd drove back with his car, and then spoke to Daddy again from the driver's seat.

Daddy asked him, "Where can we go to church around here? Anything close by?"

"Oh, there are four or five of them within a mile from here in either direction, and a big Catholic church and Mormon temple on the other edge of town. You're welcome to attend the Bible church with me and my family! I want you to meet them, anyway."

"That's pretty good news," Daddy said on the way into the house. "Six or seven churches in a town of less than 3,500 population."

"Yeah, Daddy," Thomas interjected, "but I saw when we drove through town, there are two or three beer gardens here, too, just like back in Urbandale."

***

Todd had suggested he meet us in the parking lot on our first Sunday at Chaparral Bible Church. He and his family were already there when we arrived, and that made us feel more comfortable.

Melissa Alverson, his wife, was a small-boned woman with dark, Spanish eyes and sort of warbling voice. She was such a warm and friendly person; we could see why they made a good couple.

She went directly toward Mama first. "Matilda! We finally get to meet you!" She gave Mama a hug. "Is everything going okay at your house? I hope you don't mind my poking around in there before you came. I just wanted to make sure nothing crawled in there and died since we closed it up!"

"Oh, it was fine! Much better than we expected," Mama said, returning her hug as well as her warm smile. Melissa scurried off to meet all of my aunts, and I heard Mama whisper to Margaret, "Now I know who was sweet enough to wash our curtains, and get rid of all the dust before we came."

Lou had come around their bus to meet her, too. Another hug and even tearful delight took Lou by surprise. Melissa's dark eyes swept over the group of Alverson youngsters waiting there together in neatly pressed Sunday clothes.

"The children all look so nice, and well-behaved," Melissa said. "We can't wait to spend some time with you and get acquainted!"

Aunt Molly and Aunt Vera had come to join us, and Melissa hugged them too, saying, "We'd like to have you sit near us, if you can. That's why we arrived a few minutes early."

"By the way," Todd was telling Daddy and Uncle Tommy. "We have Sunday School after worship service. You'll get used to the routine."

In Sunday school, we saw some of the same children we'd seen at the park the day we arrived. None of them were rude to us, but only two of the children smiled at us warmly like Todd and Melissa did.

One of these was Ginny, the girl who had introduced herself that day at the park; and the other was a girl named Jackie, who spoke to me right after we entered the Sunday school class, and asked if she could sit by me. She told me she lived just around the corner from us, on Old Alverson Road.

After church, Melissa and Todd asked Mama if next Sunday would be too soon to have a get-acquainted picnic in our honor, at the park. "We could make it a potluck, about an hour after church, so we'll have time to change and get our dishes of food."

Mama looked at Lou and she nodded her approval. "We'll be there," Mama said. We all tried not to reveal the little bit of trepidation we felt, wondering how this reunion would go.

CHAPTER 8

On Tuesday, I was sitting on our front steps when my cousin Betsey came over from next door. She asked if I'd like to play ball and jacks after she'd finished an errand for her parents.

"Sure," I said, "as long as it doesn't get too hot out. The shade from the house will be gone by noon. What kind of errand?"

Betsey had some papers under her arm, and held one out to show me.

"I have to deliver business letters to your mama and daddy, and to the other aunts and uncles. You want to come along?"

"Sure." I followed her to our front door.

"I'm supposed to knock," she said as I led her in. "Just pretend you heard me knocking, and you answered the door."

She tapped lightly on the door frame. I turned and said, "Hello? May I help you?"

"May I speak to your mother or father?"

"Please come in. I'll go and see."

Daddy came into the room from the bathroom, and I said, "Daddy, there's somebody here to see you."

"Uncle Ted, I have an important message for you, from my parents."

She handed it to him and waited for him to read it. Mama appeared from the kitchen, and he began to read the typewritten letter aloud:

Dear Ted and Matilda;
Molly and I would like to suggest that we have the first of our business meetings at the inn on Thursday, at 2:00 p.m.
Our agenda could be to elect officers and assign positions, at least on a temporary basis, so that we can divide up the initial responsibilities for various functions, and invite each person to bring in some ideas to the next meeting about that particular department of the new company. We believe we will accomplish more by starting out with some sort of orderly meeting, rather than just engaging in general discussion of this project.
I am inclined to think we would all benefit by having a telephone installed in our homes, as well as one at the inn itself.
Please let me know if you cannot make it to this meeting.
Have a good day.
Howard E. Borden

Daddy grinned at Mama. "A little bit formal, but it does sound like a good idea."

"It's an excellent idea. Otherwise we're going to be all talking at once, trying to make suggestions, or ask questions. Howard really is good at this sort of thing."

Daddy took a pencil out of the desk and scribbled a note: "WE'LL BE THERE."

"Here you are, Betsey. You're a pretty good

delivery girl. Keep up the good work!"

"Thank you, Uncle Ted. And Rosemary's my assistant!" We ran off to deliver the other two important letters.

"I think having a family business is going to be fun!" Betsey remarked.

"Me, too. Except that my job is probably going to be mostly at home. I have to help watch my little brother, and start doing household chores, with my sister Janet."

"Well, I'm the youngest, so I won't be doing any babysitting; but my Mama is starting to teach me to clean the bathroom and stuff. We can still do our delivery service sometimes, though. And Mama says if I learn to fold towels neatly, I might be able to help with the hotel laundry, as well as our own."

"Hey, when we go to the other houses, maybe we could see if Donna Jean and Berta Lynn want to play jacks with us. Donna Jean's got cement steps on her porch. A lot easier to bounce a ball on."

"Okay, but don't talk to them about that until I present the letter to the grown-ups. My daddy made me promise to do it just a certain way."

"Did your daddy work in an office or somethin' before? He sure seems smart about this stuff."

"Oh, yes. And so did my mama. She was a secretary in a county office, and my daddy was an accountant at the bank. He had to wear a white shirt and tie everyday, and carry a briefcase."

"He must have gone to school a long time!"

"They both did – they met in college!"

I was so impressed by this new information that

I went home later that day and told my mama all about it.

"Yes, I know, Dear," was all she said, at first. But I could tell she was thinking about it.

"Don't rave about this too much in front of your father, though, Rosemary. He's very sensitive about his own lack of education. But, you know what? Your daddy is a very smart man, and he has learned more than you think from just his own reading and life experiences."

I knew it was true, because Daddy always had a lot of books around, and when Mama worked the crossword puzzles in the newspaper, she often asked for Daddy's help when she got stuck. He usually knew the answer. The only thing Daddy didn't like to do was to manage his paycheck. It was always Mama who worked out a budget, and Daddy stuck to it faithfully.

* * *

Mama finally got to go grocery shopping. She bought some things that would be easy for Janet and me to make for lunch, like bologna for sandwiches and canned chicken noodle soup. But for Saturday and Sunday dinners, we would have chicken and dumplings, or Mama's pot roast with golden potatoes cooked along with it.

Daddy opened up a bank account downtown that day, and Mama suggested he keep out five hundred dollars to buy a family car. He bought a station wagon that could seat ten people. It could fit three people in front, two in the middle and five in the back seat, "As long as none of us get too fat," he said.

Back in Michigan, in our old Chevrolet, Tory and I had to sit on somebody's lap on the way to church, but we were getting too big for that.

Daddy also arranged to have a man put in the first telephone we had ever had. It was a party line, and we needed to wait to hear four short rings before we could answer it.

Mama and Daddy did our school shopping with the new royal blue station wagon, taking the boys in one trip and the girls in another.

Mama didn't know what children in New Mexico wore to school, but Margaret and Carrie had searched through the Sears Catalogue and found some things they liked.

In the store, we were glad we didn't see many of the sack dresses or blouses without collars we had seen so much during the war. We picked out full skirts with gathered waistlines. The older girls wanted to find pleated wool skirts like they saw in the catalogue, but Mama said the wool would be too warm for this climate, and the pleats were too hard to iron all the time.

Margaret used some of her own money to buy a Spanish, off-the-shoulder blouse, like the girl who visited Robby had worn, and a light-weight red skirt with a ruffle at the hemline.

She also bought a two-piece business suit, so she could apply for a part-time office job. That's what she had done before she went to work in the defense plant. She would still help some in the inn after it opened. Margaret found some real nylon stockings, too, so she wouldn't have to wear leg makeup anymore.

Mama bought us all some bobby sox and two-toned saddle shoes, and Scottish plaid skirts – they did have pleats, but just a few wide ones, that were easier to press. She bought me a pink and white gingham dress and a Kelly-green skirt with brass buttons at the waist, and two jumpers. And for Sunday, a purple linen suit, with a pert little black hat and purse to go with it. We bought notebooks and paper, and pencil boxes and rulers to start school.

The elementary school was about a half mile away – the same two-story, red brick school Daddy and Tommy saw near the former site of their old two-room schoolhouse. The sprawling high school and junior high was about a block further, with a football field next to that.

Cousin Todd said there were about 500 kids in the Catholic school, across town, and about 2,000 now in the Kindergarten through twelfth grade in the Chaparral Public Schools district – about 40 kids in each classroom! A lot more than the 60 students in the old school that Daddy's uncles started, forty years before.

Betsey, Donna Jean, and I would almost certainly be in the same class, so that would take some of the "new kid" fright out of it; at least I hoped it would. If the rumor was true, that half of the student body would be our relatives, I would probably have met some of them already, at church and at the big family picnic Todd was planning in our honor, this Sunday.

CHAPTER 9

Aunt Lou stopped by one day to ask if I could watch Lucy Belle at the inn while she attended the family business meeting.

"My girls are going to watch Anna Mae and Terry at home, but I want to bring the baby over there and set up the playpen in the back room. You can play with her for awhile, and then put her in there for her nap."

I quickly agreed. I loved going to the inn, and was curious about what went on in these business meetings. I wished I were old enough to work there myself, especially in the restaurant.

I went to get my journal, for something to do if Lucy Belle took a good nap. Mama had already bought me another journal, and I was filling it up real fast. I wanted to put all of this exciting stuff down, because I might want to write a book about it someday. That's what I wanted to be when I grew up – a real author, like Louisa May Alcott or Mark Twain.

The meeting started right at two. The grown-ups had arrived a few at a time. Tommy and Lou had arrived first, with me and the baby. They rang the bell once and then used their own key to enter, just as Robby was about to let us in.

This time, Robby was ready for us. His hair was combed and his clothes were pressed. He greeted us all politely and asked Tommy if he would like him to put two tables together for the meeting. Tommy helped him do this, placing eight chairs around and setting out some note pads and pencils for each person.

The others arrived soon, and everybody noticed that the living/dining area was now spotless. The plush blue and red Navajo carpeting had been vacuumed thoroughly, and all of the tables were cleared and polished.

The light, knotty pine walls displayed several framed photographs of Thurmond's family in the early days, and they were able to find Grandpa Ted and Grandma Ellen among them, and two children with them, which we knew must be daddy and Uncle Tommy.

Carrying out the Southwestern theme was a painting of an Indian on a horse, another of Geronimo, and another of an Indian princess. There was a big sombrero and an Indian style rug, in bright colors, hung on one wall, and a long shelf with pottery on another.

Robby offered to show us the apartment he and his wife lived in, and this was decorated quite differently. On the pink and blue walls were paintings of fashionable ladies and gentlemen of the 1920s, just about the time this house was built, he said. There was a small kitchen and a nice davenport and chairs. There was one bedroom, and also a fold-out Murphy bed in the living room for company.

Just before two o'clock, the adults went out to sit at the tables. I took Lucy Belle to the back room, where Tommy had set up a rocker and a playpen, with a few of the baby's favorite toys. With the door to the hall open, I could hear most of what the grown-ups were saying.

"Molly made some coffee," Howard said. "It'll be ready in a few minutes, if anybody wants some. We'll just go ahead and start. First, does anybody disagree with Todd's idea of a hotel/restaurant combination?"

Nobody disagreed, and he continued.

"Okay, there's eight of us here. Why don't we start by everybody jotting down eight jobs we'll have to do, on a regular basis, and then we'll compare the lists. Okay?"

"'Nother words, eight job titles to operate this place," Uncle Tommy said.

"Right."

I heard silence and then scratching as people started writing things down.

After fifteen minutes had passed, Howard said, "Is everybody finished?"

"Yeah," said Tommy. "Except that I thought of twelve jobs, not eight."

"That's okay. We've got older kids that could take on some responsibility, too," Lou said.

I started to rock the baby, and she put her thumb in her mouth and closed her eyes right away. Now I could hear a little better, but could not write until I gently put Lucy Belle down for her nap.

I couldn't hear every word that followed, but I was able to write most of the main jobs down in my journal:

Finance Manager/Accountant/Bookkeeper
Hospitality Manager, for hotel guests
Maintenance Manager
Housekeeping Manager (incl. Laundry)
Supplies Manager (incl. Purchasing)
Head Cook/Food Manager
Assistant Cook and Dish Crew Manager
Head Waiter/Manager of Table Service
Bus Boy, Waitress, Bell Hops, Dishwasher
Sanitation Manager
Historian & Advertising Manager
Assistant Grounds Keeper

"Sounds good," Daddy said. "Should we vote on these positions, or just volunteer, or what?"

Vera suggested, "How about if we first find out who would like to volunteer for certain jobs, and then if there's more than one, take a vote."

"Everybody agree with that method? Raise your hand if you do," Howard said.

Must be they all raised their hands, because by the end of the meeting, it seemed they had easily divided these responsibilities, with no disagreements or complaints. They all had their own department to manage, and would talk about assigning the young people later.

Uncle Howard was to be the Finance Manager and Bookkeeper; Ed Rawlings in charge of Maintenance; and my daddy the Hospitality Manager.

Uncle Tommy would be Manager of Purchasing and Supplies; Aunt Molly, the Head Cook; Aunt Lou the Assistant Cook and Dishwashing Manager; Aunt Vera, Manager of Hotel Housekeeping; and my mama, the Head Waitress. The young people would be hired for the other jobs, Howard said, and continued.

"Now, as the new Finance Manager, I have to ask: What kind of financing are we going to have for this venture? Is everybody willing to invest some money here, to get started?"

"How much do we need?" Tommy asked.

"I'd say about sixteen thousand in the account before we even open the doors. And we might have to invest some more later."

Daddy said, "I figured that. That's what Grandma had in mind when she left us the cash. And then we'll have to all work like beavers to get us going, so we can expect to start making a living wage, eventually."

"All eight of us should vote on this one, too. Can we have a show of hands?"

There was sort of a long pause this time. It must have been a little more slowly this time that all hands were raised.

"Great! Let's meet again on Tuesday, and bring in four thousand per couple to put into the account. Meeting adjourned."

CHAPTER 10

There were 204 people at the Alverson picnic that Sunday. Todd explained that there were always a lot of people who didn't make it when they had these reunions, either because of illness or previous commitments, or just lack of interest.

"I don't know where we'd put them all, if they all showed up. I only sent fliers to the families who are direct descendents of Thurmond," he said.

"Both Thurmond and Elizabeth had brothers and sisters who followed them to New Mexico; and then there were in-laws who came when their daughters or sons married Alversons and moved here. So there are almost as many townspeople now who are somehow related, but don't carry the name of Alverson."

Cars were parked down the street in every direction, and there would not have been enough tables for everyone, if most of them had not brought their own folding tables and chairs. Almost every inch of ground was covered, and getting around between tables was not easy.

Todd stood on top of one of the tables to speak to the crowd through a megaphone.

"Howdy, everybody, and welcome! I think we've all found a spot to set up our tables, now. There are three tables in the center, over here, where we're putting dishes to pass, and if you still have more food, you might have to just pass it around your own table.

"Before we say grace, I want to introduce the folks who've just arrived in the area, and then I'd like somebody from each main branch to introduce your family.

"The newcomers are the family of Thurmond's oldest son, Ted Alverson, who is now deceased. They came in from Michigan about two weeks ago. We'll introduce Thomas Alverson's descendants, then Tyrone's, and on down the line."

Mama and the Aunts brought their dishes to the serving tables, but they had to bring some of it back for lack of space. It looked like everybody had brought too much.

Todd used the megaphone, now, to start the introductions. He asked us to stand up when our name was called, and said, "If you're able to climb up onto the picnic bench, even better.

"First, we want to welcome Ted and Ellen's oldest son, Tommy Alverson, and his wife, Lou." Tommy took the megaphone so he could introduce his own nine children: Trace, Virginia, Trent, Theo, Mary Lou, Donna Jean, Terry, Anna Mae, and Lucy Belle. He lifted the baby up when he got to her.

"Say, 'Pleased to meet you all.'" Lucy bowed her head shyly, and the group laughed.

Then it was my daddy's turn. He introduced my mama (Matilda Alverson), and us eight kids: Margaret, Thomas, and Teddy the Third, who we call Teddy Cooper; Carrie, Tim, and Janet; then me (Rosemary); and finally Tory.

"Here's Ted and Ellen's oldest daughter, who was born here in New Mexico," Todd said. "Molly, and her husband, Howard Borden." Molly introduced Gloria, Tucker, and Betsey.

After that Todd welcomed Vera and her husband, Ed Rawlings, and Vera introduced my cousins Caroline, Edward Jr., Loretta, Berta Lynn, Jim, Mickey, and Donald.

I whispered to Margaret, "Why don't Vera's boys start with a T, like all the other Alverson boys?" Margaret whispered back, "Because Uncle Ed didn't want it that way."

Todd's father, Tyrone, was the oldest man there. He introduced Todd and his three sisters, and Todd presented his wife, Melissa, and their three teenagers, Rachel, Trevor and Rebecca. Todd's sisters introduced their small families, and they passed the megaphone on to the descendents of Thomas, Trent, Tad, Rena, Sarah, Arvella, and Minnie.

Among Tad's grandchildren was our caretaker, Robby, and my new friend, Ginny. I looked for

Carol, the unfriendly redhead I had met in the park. It turned out the family had quite a few red-haired people. I learned later that Grandma Elizabeth had red hair until it turned silver later on. It was Thomas Peter who had passed the lovely red locks down through his family, through Thomas Quincy, to Carol.

Then Cousin Todd led them into the singing prayer, "Be present at our table, Lord …"

As soon as the grace was done, some of the ladies hurried to take the tin-foil off the hot foods. Not that they would be likely to cool very quickly in the sweltering heat of the day.

With the park so crowded, people did not circulate much once they had their meal in front of them, so conversation was mostly between people who already knew each other.

Then Cousin Todd went back for seconds, inviting others to do so. When he had finished, he got his banjo out of his car, and brought Melissa's Spanish guitar at the same time.

Uncle Tommy and Daddy took the cue, and went for their guitars and Margaret's mandolin. Soon others had their instruments out, and Todd had begun to play one of his family's favorites tunes, "Since Jesus came into my heart …"

Dozens of Alversons, whom we had never met before today, apparently shared our love for music enough that they "just happened" to have their instruments along with them.

The afternoon was filled with song – duets, three-part harmonies, and music that everyone, at every age, felt free to sing along with. Whether you were a guitar-picker, a spectator calling out another song to try, or just a quiet foot-tapper, it was obvious that some ice had been broken, and this form of communication had begun to bring us a little bit closer to our roots – and each other.

I didn't play an instrument, but I loved to sing with my family. Especially today, when there must have been a hundred voices joining in. It made me think of that word again; what was it? *Rhapsody.* I would always remember this day, and would hear this music in my dreams for years to come.

***

Mama and Daddy sat talking at the kitchen table one evening, while I worked on my journal just around the corner. I heard them say that the family had brought in sixteen thousand dollars with which to begin the hotel and restaurant business in Grandma Elizabeth's big house.

I heard Daddy reading aloud from their copy of the written plans. It was agreed that each individual partner would own 1/8 of Alverson Inn. None of them would draw a wage or salary for their work in the company until the majority agreed that income and profits were enough to cover it, and then it would be in equal amounts.

Daddy said it would take about a year until they could start taking a salary. That meant we would be living on the inheritance at first, and had to save a lot of that for business expenses.

Right away, they would need to pay for a counter for checking in guests; a new grill and deep fryer, with an exhaust system, for the kitchen; and a Mimeograph machine for the office. Molly had asked for a soda fountain and malt machine for her ice cream treats.

The next part was even more interesting to me. Any of the kids, 15 and older, who worked for the inn, would be paid 50 cents an hour, plus tips, if they did a good job. Again I wished I was old enough to work there. That much money would buy a lot of art supplies and journals!

There were about a dozen young people old enough to work at the inn, as waiters or waitresses, bus boys and bellhops, and grounds keeper assistants. They had made Virginia a Sanitation Manager, and Trace would be the Advertising Manager and also the Historian. He would introduce our guests to the history of the area and of our family. Trace was given an advertising budget and would be allowed pretty much free rein on how to do his job.

Aunt Molly had been chosen as Head Cook because, in addition to quality home cooking, she had a knack for gourmet foods and attractive presentation that would be an asset for the inn. Aunt Lou would handle the new grill and would keep the dishwashing going with the help of the busboys, Thomas and Ed Jr., who would get them ready to wash and put them away.

Mama had a little waitress experience before she worked as a wool presser, and Margaret had worked in a diner while she was in Chicago, so they would teach Carrie and Tommy's boy, Trent, the proper ways to serve customers. Aunt Vera's daughter, Caroline, could help run Molly's soda fountain and make coffee.

Uncle Tommy would be in charge of purchasing, and bringing in the supplies, both for the restaurant and lodging part of the business.

And Daddy, because of his experience in a big hotel in St. Louis those many years before, would be responsible for everything the hotel customers experienced when they came to stay at Alverson Inn. Hospitality, he said, included welcoming guests, checking them in and out, meeting their needs while they were here, and everything else that affected their impression of the inn. He would train two 16-year-old bellhops – Tommy's boy, Theo; and my brother, Teddy Cooper – to give excellent service, "just like downtown." He would take reservations over the new telephone, and "jump through hoops" to accommodate the guests. If necessary, he would pick up customers at the bus or train station.

During the school year, they would just have to do without the daytime bellhops and two of the waitresses, so the adults would have to work very hard if there were busy days. At least they would have some help with the dinner hour, and on weekends. They decided to close the restaurant until 2:00 p.m. on Sundays, and then alternate between staff members at the checkout counter so that nobody would have to stay home from church more than once a month.

Howard had already bought the new Mimeograph machine that afternoon to make copies. Trace planned to make a typewritten menu, with prices, and would include it in an advertising flier announcing an opening date two weeks after Labor Day. Tory would help take the fliers house to house in Chaparral, and Trace would also mail them to businesses in Socorro and Deming.

Howard was making a tiny office out of a storage closet. He and his son, Tucker, brought over a desk that had come with their house, and had been able to buy a four-drawer oak file cabinet from the Horton Law Office.

I put down my journal and wandered into the kitchen to get a cold drink of water. Mama and Daddy went on talking while she started to peel potatoes for supper.

"So it might be years before we really have an income from the inn," Mama said.

"That's right," Daddy replied. "Any business takes time to build up, and if we don't spend the money to run a quality place, people just won't come back. Grandma knew this; that's why she left us the money, not just the property."

Mama checked her meatloaf and got the potatoes boiling on the stove. She wiped her hands on her apron and sat down next to him.

"We'll need to make a budget," she said.

Daddy took a notebook out of his shirt pocket and asked me to lend him my pencil. He put them both in front of Mama, grateful that she had mentioned it. Daddy hated to wrestle with numbers, and Mama was better at it.

"How much have we got left in the bank?"

"About nineteen thousand now," he said.

"Suppose we plan to live on the same amount we earned back in Michigan? That should be more than enough, because we don't have any rent to pay here."

"And remember, Matilda, some of the kids will be working for pay – fifty cents an hour. They oughta be able to buy more of their own clothes and other things, and should still be able to save a couple of dollars a week."

Mama turned the burner down so nothing would boil over. "Let's put two years' living expenses in a separate account, and let the rest of it be our investment funds." She wrote down some more numbers. "We should be fine. We shouldn't have to live in poverty or anything."

* * *

The grownups all worked hard to get the inn ready. Mama made sky blue and white uniforms for the bellhops and waitresses on her treadle sewing machine. As the kitchen staff worked out the menu, they let the rest of us eat meals there, so they could practice. Other than that, children who were too young to hire usually stayed at home, with the 13- and 14-year-olds in charge.

So now I was Janet's helper, and we took care of that big house and our 9-year old brother and received an allowance of twenty-five cents a week for each year of our age. It got pretty tiring, and I was glad school would be starting soon.

CHAPTER 11

I looked at myself in the bathroom mirror one morning and grimaced. No matter what I did to try to make myself look better, it was hopeless.

Last year, I loved school, and books, and my teacher, and recess, and never gave a thought to my appearance. This year, on the first day at Chaparral Elementary, in sixth grade, it seemed critically important to look my best.

We girls had our showers the night before so the boys could take theirs in the morning, and Mama had shampooed my hair, dried it with a towel, then brushed it until it shined. This morning she had brushed it again before she put in my braids.

I brushed my teeth hard with my brand-new yellow toothbrush and real toothpaste, but my teeth still looked ugly. My two front teeth were too wide, and there was no way to hide my "overbite." I had tried many times to keep my chin out enough to make the upper and lower teeth meet, but it just looked like a foolish clown face, so I stopped trying.

Mama told me once that I had a beautiful smile, and pointed out that Carrie had the same wide front teeth that I had, and she did. But, on her, it looked good. Carrie was fifteen and pretty. I was eleven and awkward, and I didn't want to go to school.

The pink and white gingham dress, with its round white collar and belted waist, had looked pretty the day we bought it, but now I wondered if it would seem old-fashioned or plain. And I looked so flat-chested in it. My body had just begun to change, and I yearned to look like a young lady instead of a little girl.

My cousin Betsey had matured sooner than I had, and it seemed my sister, Janet, only two years older, had been wearing brassieres forever.

Toby banged on the bathroom door. "Come on, Rosie! I have to go bad!"

"Okay, I'm coming!" I put away my toothbrush and tried to wipe the front of my dress with a washcloth, where I had splashed a little. I wondered if it would leave a spot, right where I did not want to attract attention.

I went out to the kitchen and shook my head when Carrie offered me cocoa and toast and an orange for breakfast. I didn't want to take the chance of more spots, and besides, I was too nervous to be hungry.

Mama had gone to work at the inn right after she braided my hair, and I vaguely remembered her saying I should eat before putting my dress on. Next time, I promised myself, I would leave my housecoat on until everything else was done.

I picked up my new Judy Garland lunch box and followed Janet out the door. As I waited by Betsey's house so we could walk together, Jackie, the girl from Old Alverson Road who had been nice to me in Sunday School, came around the corner and called to me.

I turned around and waved, noticing that she was wearing a wartime sack dress, like the ones I wore back in Michigan. I felt guilty for fretting about my brand new outfit.

Her "Good morning!" was so bright and friendly, I forgot about my worries and joined her, just as Betsey came out of her house.

We all walked with a lively step, swinging our lunch boxes and skipping lightly over the paved road to get on the left side, as we'd been taught, facing the occasional car and stepping aside onto the gravel when one came along.

Janet and our cousin, Mary Lou, walked a short distance ahead of us and I watched them turn off at the combined Junior High and High School building, where they would begin eighth grade today. Janet nudged her glasses more tightly to her face and brushed back her long, auburn hair as they entered the building, looking confident in her longer, "new look" skirt and forest green cotton sweater. Janet never seemed to have gone through an awkward moment, having always had perfect teeth, delightful dimples and beautiful hair.

We entered our sixth grade classroom and met Miss Beach, a cheerful, soft-spoken teacher with salt-and-pepper hair. We were allowed to choose our own desk, which we would keep during the entire school year. Betsey sat in front of me, and Jackie, whom the teacher called Jacqueline, slid in behind me. I lifted the desk top and put in my lunch box, taking out the new pencils first and placing them carefully beside it.

Moments later, Ginny Alverson took the desk beside me. Carol sat in front of her, whispering something to Ginny and pointing slyly at Jackie.

Ginny wrinkled her brows in disapproval of whatever her cousin had said to her. Then she threw us a half-smile, and Carol turned her back.

Carol looked stunning today in a crisp, cotton sundress with a matching short-sleeved jacket. Tiny white flowers bordered the pastel green dress and open jacket. Her soft red curls hung down her back, seemingly untouched by the dry summer breeze or the long walk – longer than ours, because now I knew she lived in one of the elaborate homes farther down Alverson Drive.

She was a daughter of Uncle Thomas Quincy Alverson, who published the county's daily newspaper. Thomas Q had kept part of his father's ranch, which included Grandpa Ted's old property; had torn down two houses; and then had a more prestigious home and stables built. Carol's creamy complexion and straight teeth, as well as her stand-offish manner, nearly set me back to the depression that I'd started out the day with.

But my friends, the nice teacher, and the lovely day bolstered my spirits considerably. I looked forward to the school year ahead, and ended my day praising the Lord for bountiful blessings since we arrived in New Mexico.

***

One night a few weeks later, just after the inn had officially opened, I couldn't get to sleep. Our bedroom door was open a crack, and I overheard my parents talking in the kitchen.

"What do you think they're going to do, Ted? Would they really leave, do you think?"

"He may be just blowing off steam," Daddy replied. I wondered who they were talking about, and why they sounded so worried.

"Ed's used to getting a paycheck every Friday night; something to show for his hard work," Daddy continued.

"Well, I know we were all expecting a little more business by now; but they've got the majority of their money still in the bank, like we do. They're not in any danger of going broke!"

"True, but Ed's always been a worrier, Matilda. You know that!"

"Maybe so, but they're so much better off already than they were back home. Like you said at the meeting, companies are not built overnight. That's why Grandma left the money to live on, instead of just the property. She knew it would take time to turn a profit."

"What's he so worried about? I figure as long as we set a limit of investment – like keeping a thousand in the bank in case we ever have to fold up and go back -- we're still better off to keep plodding away, 'specially when each month is a little better!"

"Vera's out of sorts, too. I just wish they wouldn't grumble in front of the young folks. Especially the ones that are out of school, and could get other jobs."

"What's all this about Tom's boy, Trent? What's so bad about waiting on tables? He's getting paid for it, for Pete's sake!"

"Lou says it's that girl he's still writing to in Ann Arbor. He wants to go back there and get married. He says he can't expect her to come here, if all he has to offer is a part-time job waiting on tables, in a place that might shut down before he ever gets to be full time."

"Does Tommy know about all this?" Daddy grumbled. "He hasn't said a word to me about Trent leaving, just that the boy wasn't quite satisfied with his job. Shoot, he's only 19 years old! Kinda' young to be getting married!"

"I was younger than that when you married me," Mama said, quietly.

"That's different. I was 22, and had a full time job, at least. This is a great opportunity for those kids. They can learn more here than at any business college."

"I hope they don't go – not so soon, without giving it a chance," Mama said. I could hear the sadness in her voice. "I don't think Vera wants to leave, but she will if Ed insists. We'd not only be losing a good maintenance man and housekeeper; we'd be losing close family members!"

"Dog gone it! We all came here together, to build a family enterprise!"

Their voices went on until past midnight. I lay in my bed, hating to hear them in such a troubled mood, and hating the possibility of our family being scattered even more than before.

Sure enough, Ed and Vera and their family left, and Trent also went back to Michigan. Everyone else was even busier now, and my parents and my sisters and brothers were always bringing their work home with them. On the phone, at the kitchen table, even on the way to church, I heard snatches of job-related complaints or comments.

It occupied their minds so much that I didn't feel free to tell them about a program at school that I would be performing in, or a mean trick a boy had played on my friend Jackie. I knew they all worked hard, and had important problems to work out. But did they know, on nights like this, it could be hard to be 11 sometimes, too?

CHAPTER 12

A week before I turned 12, I became a woman.

I was terrified, worried and ashamed. My sister Janet had told me, when I asked about the box of pads she always kept in our closet, that when you get to be a teenage girl, you bleed once a month – unless you were a bad girl, like one she heard about in Michigan, who let a boy touch her, and she had a baby when she was only 14.

But if you were decent, it was a good thing, Janet had said, because it meant you had become a woman, and could have children if you got married.

It didn't seem like such a good thing right now – it was uncomfortable and embarrassing. I had to go and borrow the pads from Janet, and whisper so nobody else would hear me. Janet said we could never talk about it, or our brothers might find out. She gave me some safety pins and told me how to use the pads.

I didn't say anything to Mama, but she saw the stains on my pajamas and sheet while doing the laundry the next day. She seemed sad and embarrassed, too, and asked me if I knew how to use the pads. I said yes, and she said, "Good. I love you, Rosie." That was all she said, but soon I found a new box of pads on my closet shelf.

Going to school was harder on these days, and I didn't tell anybody what had happened to me, even Betsey or Jackie. Even when it had let up and I felt better, I was still terrified if a boy spoke to me, or looked at me without saying anything. One day a boy brushed past me trying to catch up with his friend in the hallway, and I worried for two weeks that I might be pregnant. I had to be more careful from now on.

It was months later that I finally confided in Margaret, who had gotten married in the summer. She was over for a visit, and while Mama was out of the room, I asked her a few questions about being a woman.

She gave me a clear and simple explanation of the reproductive system, how a husband and wife make love to each other, and how sometimes God blesses them with a child nine months later. This set my mind at ease a little bit. I began wondering what it might be like to be a wife and mother.

Margaret's wedding had been beautiful, and Derron was such a nice Christian man. He was working as a counselor at the Christian Academy in Deming. He got along well with our family, and they visited often. I wondered if I'd ever find someone special of my own.

Then I asked Margaret, "Do you think I could marry Trace someday?"

"Honey, you can't marry your first cousin!"

So many rules. How many nice boys were there in Chaparral that were *not* my cousins? What if I never found anyone to marry? Growing up was starting to seem scary.

But there turned out to be advantages, too, to my new status as a woman. My last years' school clothes were getting tight on me, and I had begun to fill out a bit. Maybe I could buy some new clothes! But when I asked Mama, she said we had to go back to wearing hand-me-downs, because business was still slow.

This wasn't so bad, though, because I got Janet's stylish wardrobe, including her "new look" ballet-length dresses, before any of the other girls in my class had them. Janet got Carrie's outgrown clothes, and Carrie got to buy a new wardrobe with her earnings from working part-time at the inn. I gave my old clothes to my friend, Jackie. She looked better in them than I had. The gingham dress didn't make her look flat on top, at all.

* * *

Seventh grade was a little more fun than the sixth, but I still missed having Mama home when I got home from school. Betsey and I started telling each other things that we normally would have told our mothers. Both of us had big sisters at home, but that wasn't the same.

We still ate our evening meal at the Alverson Inn, but by now there were usually dozens of other diners.

Mama kept busy waiting on tables, cleaning, and doing laundry at the inn, and Carrie helped her whenever she wasn't in school.

Janet shared a room with me now, using Margaret's old twin bed. Because she was older, she got to pick the spot by the window. I didn't think it was fair – it wasn't my fault I was the second-youngest in the family!

I asked Mama if I could start helping in the restaurant, and she said she would think about it. For now I had to just help Janet at home.

I was surprised at how soon I had the chance to be a part of the inn – a bigger part, even, than I had bargained for.

***

The high school was closed one day for teachers' meetings. I decided to drop in at the inn and see if I could eat lunch there.

It was a good thing I did, because the place was packed with customers when I arrived. Mama and Carrie were overwhelmed.

Seeing people who had just come in, I grabbed a pad of guest checks from behind the counter without asking, and began taking orders.

The first customers wanted burgers and fries and chocolate malts. My whole family had been taught how to make the malts, so we could make our own when we went over there.

I clipped the guest order on Aunt Lou's string as I'd seen Mama do; grabbed three portions of fries out of the freezer and dumped them into an empty fry basket to dunk into the bubbling oil; then set about making three chocolate malts on the new machine.

Mama's chin dropped when she saw what I was doing, but she was too grateful to object.

"You'd better put an apron on, at least," she called out as she passed, and pointed to a stack on a shelf. I put one on and hurried back to complete the order.

When the malts were about done, I found a blue plastic tray, then stopped to pick up the burgers Aunt Lou had already wrapped and marked for me, with the golden fries in their paper nests.

"Don't forget ketchup!" Mama reminded me, pointing to the packets of condiments behind me.

I placed the food carefully in front of each guest and said, "I'll be right back with your malts." That finished, I turned to a man at the next table. "Have you been waited on, Sir?"

"No, I haven't. I'd like the hot beef special, please. And coffee with cream." Clipping the new order on the string, I hurried to the coffee maker and filled up a cup. Now, if I could just get it to his table without spilling it.

I made it, somehow. Before I knew it, I had served the hot beef special, three more coffees, two bowls of chili, and some ice water.

"We're fine now, Rosie," Mama said. "Why don't you make a lunch for yourself and sit down?

You've earned it!"

I enjoyed the burger and chocolate malt I had for lunch, but even more, I loved the look of pride on Mama's face, and the feeling that I was old enough to actually help my family.

***

Months had passed since I'd helped with the noon-hour rush and we went back to our usual routine. I had just come in the door from school, when the telephone rang. It was Mama.

"Rosemary, listen carefully. We need you to come and help clean the guest rooms. Is Janet there yet?"

"She's right here!" I handed over the phone.

"Yes, Tory's home. He's changing his clothes. Okay, I understand. 'Bye, Mama."

"Mama wants you over there right away; don't even change your clothes first," Janet said. "She will explain when you get there."

I hurried across to the inn, and Mama met me, a little breathless. Carrie was polishing the ice cream fountain, and Teddy Cooper was getting ready to vacuum the dining and living room carpet.

"We're going to be extra busy," Mama said, "and we have to be ready. An archeology convention in Socorro, in the Rio Hotel, is over-flowing – some mistake in the phone reservation, I guess. We have 16 people coming at five o'clock, so Daddy has to put up four of our rollaway cots to take up the slack. We had already done the basic cleaning, but the third floor needs dusting and polishing, and we need to put in linens and soaps for extra people. Be a good girl and help us out."

She led me to the linen closet while she went on talking.

"Do a good job, but hurry. Then we'll need you in the kitchen for a while. You said you wanted to work, so we're going to pay you by the hour while you're here."

I counted out enough towels and wash cloths for a dozen people, and then went to the supply cupboard to pick up the fragrant little soap bars with "Alverson Inn" on the wrappers. Mama brought me the cleaning supplies I would need.

I arranged everything in sets to place on the shelves below the cabinet mirrors: two big bath towels, two hand towels, and two wash cloths in each set, with soaps on top of each stack.

Then I started on the furniture. Each dresser was free of dust and shining clean when I finished, and each nightstand as well. Teddy Cooper had already vacuumed the carpets, so I just opened the windows a few inches and turned on the fan to air things out a little. Each room smelled clean and fresh when I left it.

Then I checked the third-floor bathroom, and noticed only one roll of toilet paper there, and none in the cupboard below the wash basin. I knew where they kept it in each hall closet, so I brought in a few more and then decided to shine up the chrome faucets a little more for good measure.

I hurried back downstairs just as the first few convention guests arrived, and Daddy was checking them in. Mama grabbed me as soon as I entered the kitchen.

"Rosie, I need you to put silverware on the tables. Use a paper napkin to shine each knife, spoon, and fork, and roll them in a linen napkin like so." She did the first set to demonstrate for me. "Then take them in and set them at each place setting, still tightly wrapped in the napkin." She smiled warmly. "And thanks, Honey."

After I had finished this task, I went back and helped refill salt and pepper shakers, and then brought them on a tray to set on each table. My cousin Gloria, Betsy's 15-year-old sister, was filling bread baskets, using a big linen napkin as a lining, placing the rolls and crackers on it, and then folding the napkin up over it all.

At the salad counter, Carrie showed me how to make individual salads on a dainty plate, with thin slices of tomato, long slabs of green pepper, and julienne cheese arranged on top of crispy lettuce, with little cups of Aunt Molly's special dressing placed just so on the plate. We did two dozen of these and lined them up on the little shelf made for that purpose, to await the precise moment Mama wanted them served.

Then Carrie showed me the water glasses.

"When Mama signals you for water, put two ice

cubes in each glass with these tongs, get the water from this fountain, and put them on a round tray. Be careful not to get them too full, about this far from the top." She showed me with her fingers. "A waitress will pick them up, and we don't want any water spilled on the way to the tables."

Everything went fine until I accidentally placed a tray too close to the edge of the counter, and it toppled to the floor with two water glasses on it. The loud crash and sound of glass breaking was bad enough; but the puddle of water had to be cleaned up quickly before somebody slipped and fell in it.

"I'm sorry! I'm sorry!" I wailed, and Mama came rushing toward me with her finger over her lips. "It's okay, darling," she whispered, and turned immediately to send Carrie for the mop. Seeing tears welling up, she put her arm around my shoulders. "It could happen to anyone. The customers hardly noticed."

"I'll try to be more careful," I promised.

"I know you will, dear. But, Rosie, I was just about to tell you, it's time for your break. See that little store room behind the kitchen? That's where we take our breaks." It was the same room where I used to babysit Lucy Belle. She led me toward it. "Just sit down and relax; have a Coca Cola and wait until I bring you your supper."

Later, she came with a plate of food for me and one for Gloria, who had now joined me.

"I want to tell you girls how thankful we are that

you came to help us out tonight," Mama said. "We weren't used to a full house, and I'm afraid we weren't prepared for it."

"I hope Daddy won't be mad about me causing a disturbance," I said. "I know he says everything that happens when a customer is here matters, so he will want to come back and bring a friend."

"Rosie, if I had a nickel for every time I dropped something, we'd be rich by now." She hurried back to the dining room.

Her comment about being rich reminded me that I was going to be paid fifty cents an hour while working here. Maybe I could save up for a home permanent, and wear my hair down like Carol's, instead of these pesky old braids.

The next two days were Friday and Saturday. I could come after school tomorrow, and start earlier in the day on Saturday. Having a real job was tiring, but I sure liked it better than just hanging around the house.

CHAPTER 13

I wasn't asked to work at the Inn again until the next time the hotel unexpectedly filled up, which only happened a few times a year.

The grown-ups did fix up the break room a little more, though, and said we could come over after school whenever we wanted, as long as we had our rooms picked up at home.

So, after school, Janet would wash the breakfast dishes while I took care of some of the clutter, and then we went right over to the Inn instead of waiting until dinner time. At least we got to see our parents more that way, and they could give us a short task anytime they needed to. We were "on call," Mama said. I liked that phrase; it sounded important.

We only got paid when we actually had to work, but it was fun being there anyway. We could do our school work, work jigsaw puzzles, or play one of our many paper and pencil games. Sometimes I brought my journal or sketchbook.

We had uniforms hanging on some hooks on the wall, and were right near the main floor bathroom, so it only took a few minutes to be ready to work if they ever called us.

On one of these "on call days," when I was fourteen, Mama asked me to bring a stack of fresh linens to a business man who had been there a week, and make his bed.

It made me a little nervous to have him there watching me as I tucked in the sheets the way I had been taught, nice and square at the corners, and very tight and smooth. I plumped up the pillows and was about to fold the bedspread up over them when I noticed a strange expression on the man's face.

His knitted brows quivered and his piercing eyes followed every move I made; and before I could bend to pick up the soiled linen, he approached me, standing so close to me that I nearly fell back onto the bed. He smelled of sweat and tobacco and his hair was greasy. I tried to step around him, but he blocked my way. I began to panic, and he started to talk softly as he pulled something from his shirt pocket and showed me. It was a twenty-dollar bill.

"Wouldn't you like to earn some extra cash once in awhile, to get some pretty clothes, or some jewelry?"

"For what?" I asked in a forced whisper, but by the way he was trying to press against me, I instinctively knew his intentions were bad.

I finally found my voice and yelled "No!" at the

same instant pushing forcefully past him.

He became angry. "I saw the way you strutted in here, like you owned the place today. If you don't want any, don't flaunt it, Girlie!"

I was afraid he would grab me, so I called on every ounce of strength I had to move away from him, scooped up the linens from the floor, and ran out of the room.

I ran immediately to the supply closet, stuffed the soiled linens into the chute, and leaned against the wall to get my breath. Hot tears rolled down my cheeks, and goose bumps came out on my arms. The whole scene replayed in my mind, and sent shivers down my spine.

Should I tell Mama or Daddy? What did the man mean when he said I was "flaunting" myself? Did I walk differently since I'd started to get a woman's figure?

What if my parents thought it was my fault? He was a regular paying customer. Would they believe him if he said I had behaved badly?

I decided not to tell, at least for now.

When I crawled into my own bed that evening, I prayed fervently, both for protection and forgiveness. I told myself I had probably been too proud of my changing appearance, and the man mistook my pride for an appeal for attention – the wrong kind of attention.

The only thing I ever mentioned to Mama, as a result of this dreadful experience, was that I preferred the kitchen and dining room work to taking care of the guests upstairs. Her eyes widened in surprise and curiosity, but she never did ask me if there was a problem. I don't believe the man ever came back, and I was glad.

CHAPTER 14

When I first saw Dan Cole, he was walking past our house on the way to school, with two other boys from Old Alverson Road. They were all my age, but he was a head taller and twenty pounds bulkier than his friends – wide-shouldered and barrel-chested, and carrying himself like a football player.

He wore old blue jeans and well-worn cowboy boots, and Jackie said it was because he had an after-school job at one of the ranches down the road. I found out later the ranch was my Uncle Thomas Quincy's place. Dan had large, puffy eyelids, scraggly black hair, and a jagged scar on one side of his mouth. He wore a shirt tucked in on one side and hanging out on the other; this, along with his size, made him seem like he might have been "held back" to take the ninth grade over again. But, no, according to Jackie, he was a straight A student.

I wondered why I hadn't noticed him the previous year, or the one before that. Of course, I barely noticed boys at all until this year.

I don't recall Dan ever speaking to me directly that year, but he always seemed to be showing off for his friends when I looked his way. I never would have guessed that he was actually very shy around girls.

It wasn't until our senior year of high school that I realized I had developed a crush on him.

I had a small group of friends from our church who attended football games together, went roller skating, and had barbecues and back yard parties – mainly Betsey, Jackie, Ginny, Dennis Brewer, my brother Tim, and me.

Dan Cole didn't seem to do much except work and study during his high school years. I knew little about him or his family, except that his mother had died and his father was not well. But there was something about him that I found hard to resist – and it wasn't just the fact that he wasn't related to me!

One day in the girls' restroom at school, I overheard my stuck-up cousin Carol talking about me. "Have you noticed? Rosemary has a crush on our stable boy!" I waited in the stall until I was sure everybody had gone. I felt angry and embarrassed, but the incident only made me more certain that I liked him.

I wanted Dan to ask me to the Prom, but he didn't, so I went with Ricky Diaz. This turned out to be a bad idea, because Ricky ruined the whole evening by trying to make improper advances afterward. This upset me so much that I decided to stick with just group activities for a long time and work as many nights as I could at the Inn. I would expand my hours even more, once I had finished high school.

Then we all graduated. I heard that Dan was working his way through the local college, and that his father had died. Dan was still living in his family home on Old Alverson Road, all by himself. *He must be very lonely*, I thought.

My friend Jackie lived next door to him, so, when she held a cookout on her 19th birthday, she invited him, and he came. He walked over a little late, having gone home after work to clean up. He was wearing a royal blue sport shirt that brought out the color in his heavy-lidded eyes.

For the first time, he made it a point to sit by me, and caught my eye a few times. When some of my cousins brought out their musical instruments, Dan pulled a small harmonica from his pocket and joined in the music. Later, I heard him sing out in a rich, clear voice, apparently enjoying the old-time gospel songs my cousins chose. The scar on his lip made his smile a little lopsided, but he was still very good looking.

We ate ground beef barbecues and apple pie. I never saw anybody put away so much food in one sitting! He hung around whatever side of the room I happened to be in, although he didn't say much to me at all, and it warmed my heart. This turned out to be one of the best parties I had attended in my teenage years.

A few days later, on a Sunday evening, Mama called me to the telephone.

It's for you, Rosie. Don't talk long; we're leaving for church in ten minutes."

"I won't," I said. I expected it to be Jackie, Ginny or Betsey. "Hello?"

"Well, Hello!"

When I recognized the deep, mellow voice, my heart skipped a beat.

"Hello, Dan."

"Oh, you did recognize my voice. Took you a minute, though, didn't it? Hope you're not disappointed."

"Not at all. You sound nice on the phone."

He did. I'd never realized what a nice speaking voice Dan had. Warm, even charming.

He laughed. "Well, I am nice. You just never noticed!"

"Yes I have. I noticed you at Jackie's party that night, the minute you walked in. I don't often run into you at parties."

"Well, I don't often go to many parties. Too busy working and hitting the books. But, I'm glad I went to that one."

"Did you have a good time?"

"You know I did. I should have walked you home. I turned my back for a minute, and you were gone!"

"My brother Tim was there, so he walked home with me and Betsey."

"Rosie, c'mon now!" It was my Mama.

"I have to get going. Thanks for calling."

"You got a big date tonight?"

"Just going to church with my family. You could go along, if you like."

"I have to study. Was it okay that I called?"

"Oh, yes. I'll be home in two hours. You could

call again, about 8:45 if you want to."

"We'll see. I'll try to get done by then."

I didn't know whether that was a yes or a no.

"Well, 'bye, Dan."

"'Bye now."

At 8:45 that night, the phone rang. I was right there, ready to answer quickly, not wanting to attract too much attention. I sat on the dining room floor, speaking as quietly as I could.

Again, Dan's voice appealed to me in a way I never would have expected, after all these years that he'd been around as my neighbor and classmate. I thought I had outgrown the crush I had on him, but that evening at Jackie's party had changed everything.

"Well, hello again!"

"Dan?"

"You haven't forgotten my voice already, have you? You said I sounded nice on the phone awhile ago!"

"You still do. Sorry I had to cut the conversation short, before."

"I'll forgive you, just this once."

"Did you finish your school work?"

"More or less. Probably did a poor job of it, though. I couldn't keep my mind off you, now that I finally got your attention."

"You've never called me before today."

"Well, you never even looked my way before. You've always been so busy talking to your own friends, I didn't think you'd want me to say anything to you. I'm pretty shy around girls, you know."

"You weren't so shy at Jackie's party."

"That's because you smiled at me a couple of times. At least, I think it was me you were looking at."

I laughed. "You still didn't talk to me much. But you looked like you were in a good mood, and I had fun listening to your music."

"Oh, you like music, do you? So if I wanted to come calling on you sometime, I should bring my harmonica?"

"You bet. You'd fit right into our family band! My daddy, my brothers and cousins – those were cousins of mine you were playing with at Jackie's party!"

"How about you? Do you play, too?"

"I just sing along, if I know the tune. I never learned any banjo pickin' or anything. But I can do a whole lot of foot tappin'!"

"I'll tell you what: You give me a call the next time they get in the mood to play, and I'll come over if I can." He gave me his phone number, and I wrote it down.

I decided that was a promise to visit, and a good way for my folks to get to know him. I could hardly believe this was the same Dan Cole I had seen every day since I started school in this town. I could hardly wait to see him again.

CHAPTER 15

Dan was still shy, but we were drawn to each other like bears to honey from that time on. I learned to love everything about him, from his heavy eyelids to his football-player build, even his scar; and he had a voice that I felt I had heard and responded to my entire life.

We both held down jobs five days a week, and Dan drove back and forth to the university for his morning classes and then worked at the ranch; but when I got out of work in the early evening, he was right there waiting for me.

We never stayed out late during the week because he had to study after we said goodnight. Saturday and Sunday afternoons, we could always be found together, either at my house or at the inn with the family. After dinner, we often walked through town holding hands, or drove out to a shady spot at the foot of the mountains.

I invited him to church with us, but he was always too tired, or busy studying. I tried talking to him about the Lord a few times, but I didn't want to press the point until he seemed ready. He seemed to respect my Christian values, at least.

When Mama asked me about his beliefs, I skirted the issue. "You know I would never get serious about someone who wasn't a Christian," I replied. A little voice inside told me something was wrong, but I ignored it.

Soon afterward, Dan and I were walking in the park when I brought the subject up again.

He told me his mother had been a Christian, and she had once taken his sister and him to church when his father went on an all-day fishing trip. His father was furious!

Dan said his father, Maynard Cole, had been a very strict and controlling man whose word was law in his household. As a result of the terrible scene that had followed his mother's "rebellious" behavior, he had sworn that if she ever tried any such thing again, he would burn her precious Bible with the rest of the trash.

"That's terrible," I said. "But, Dan, your Dad is gone now. There's nothing stopping you from worshipping God."

Dan shook his head. "My mother's faith didn't do her any good," he said. "She prayed and read her Bible every day after Dad went to work, but her life with him was miserable.

"I never heard my Dad compliment her about the delicious bread and pies she produced in that clunky old oven every day, or the fresh supply of clean overalls he wore to work. I never saw him give her a hug, or carry a heavy box for her, or make any kind gesture. He cried at her funeral, but by then it was too late.

"I never forgave him," he said angrily, "and I can't believe in a God who wouldn't answer the prayers of a wonderful woman like that."

When my sister Carrie got married, Dan attended the wedding with me. Actually I was in the wedding, as a bridesmaid, along with Janet, who was also engaged to be married within the year. So, I had to get there early, but Dan was my date for the big reception held right at the Alverson Inn.

The family band played that night, including the father of the bride, four brothers and two cousins. Even Margaret was coaxed into playing one song on her beautiful mandolin. It sounded wonderful, and it brought tears to my eyes. Then Dan played his harmonica, and I sang some of my favorite songs.

Daddy had let me choose a name for the ever-changing band, so it was now known as "Rhapsody."

As busy as everybody was, keeping up with the business, their other jobs or their schooling, they all took time to make music together whenever they could; so this was the only word I could think of that described how it made me feel. It was a big part of my life that I treasured, and having Dan there made it even better.

Our growing romance went on for nearly a year. Other than the matter of faith, we seemed perfect for each other. I was hopeful that I could eventually win Dan over to the Lord.

But one night, we parked a little bit too long on the deserted lane behind my house.

Dan had kissed me many times before, and I'd melted into his arms each time he held me close. I didn't remember when we had first begun to whisper sweet words of love – probably while we walked hand in hand among the foothills outside of town, or during our playful games of keep away in the park, with Dan's old tennis ball.

But never in the dark, alone in a parked car on a moonlit night. Somehow those words, whispered into my ear, set my pulse throbbing as never before, and I instinctively wound my arms around him and returned his wonderful kiss. And, for just a brief moment, Dan revealed his own passion by the sudden urgency in his embrace, and the whisper of my name.

"No, Dan!" When I started to pull away, he drew back abruptly and said, "I've got to get you home!" Annoyance, more at himself than at me, had taken over his mind. We didn't say another word until we stood at my doorstep.

Not knowing what else to say, I reminded him that the homecoming game was the following evening. "Do you still want to go?"

He nodded. "But let's not go to the dance, okay? We need to have a chance to talk about some things."

We left the athletic field right after the game, skipping the homecoming dance entirely. Instead of pulling into our driveway as usual, Dan passed our house and turned left onto Old Alverson Road, parking in his own driveway.

He turned off the ignition, and then turned to look at me intently.

"Come closer," he said at last, reaching out to gather me into his arms. He touched my cheek, and then, with strong, gentle hands, tilted my face upward so that our eyes met.

"I don't want to go on like this."

I flinched. "Are you breaking up with me?"

"I love you! I want you to be my wife!" he said, as if I should have known. "Will you marry me? Next summer, I mean, when school's out, so I can get a decent job and support us? I want to start planning the wedding now."

Stunned, I couldn't find words to give any response at all. My heart cried out that I loved him and wanted him so much that it scared me. I wanted to answer, *Yes, my darling, I will marry you and follow you to the ends of the earth*, but something stopped me.

I wanted to build a Christian home. That had always been my dream, but would Dan be able to share that with me?

"Look at me, Rose!" His words brought me back to the present, and I still didn't know how to answer him. I tried to avert his penetrating gaze, but he made me look at him.

"Dan, you know we have some issues to resolve, and I don't know if we should let things get so serious . . ."

"You don't want to marry me." He dropped his hand from my face and lowered his gaze.

"I didn't say that, Dan."

"I could hear it in your voice," he said, "and in your silence."

"Dan, you know I love you."

"I thought I knew that. All this time, you let me think you felt the same way as I did, and the minute

I mention having a future together, you pull away from me!"

I covered my eyes with my hands, and pleaded with the Lord to give me the go-ahead on this. But all I could think about is what I'd learned about marriage. The scriptures asked plainly, "What communion would a non-believer have with a believer?" I knew that a Christian marriage was the only kind I could enter.

"I can't do it, Dan. Not when you don't share my faith, my love for the Lord. I'm so sorry."

He held his hands up. "Okay, fine! Forgive me for asking!" He took his car keys out of his pocket and jammed them into the ignition. I had seen a rare display of his anger the night before, but that was directed towards himself, for nearly losing control. It was my fault, anyway, for responding so eagerly to his kisses.

Now, he had opened up his heart to me and offered me the rest of his life – and I had refused!

He tore out of the driveway, almost knocking down his mailbox. A minute later he had stopped in front of my home, and lost no time going around to open the door for me.

"Dan, please understand?" I ventured, hoping we could talk it over. But he swiftly walked me to my front door and turned to leave.

"Will I see you tomorrow night?" I asked.

He threw a glance at me over his shoulder, and said, "What's the point, Rosemary? I'm not the guy you want."

CHAPTER 16

Lonely days turned into weeks, with still no word from Dan.

Somehow, I got through each work shift at the inn, but there was no longer a spring in my step. Each evening, when the phone didn't ring by nine o'clock, I wearily crawled into bed, and then tossed and turned half the night. When I tried to pray, I couldn't find the words.

Sunrise came too early, and no longer seemed to flood the hovering mountains with glorious color and light. Even the usual Sunday afternoon gatherings with my family and friends, and the music we made, had lost their appeal for me without the resonance of Dan's harmonica or his sweet, clear voice singing out.

I'd been so sure I was doing the right thing, dating Dan even though I knew he wasn't a Christian. I thought God would use me to win him over. He had shown some genuine interest in the Christian music we played, and had never hung around with the rough crowd, or used bad language that they thought was so cool.

I wasn't expecting his proposal, and couldn't believe he would bolt and run when I couldn't accept right away. Didn't he know he was the only man I wanted to spend my future with?

Oh, how I wanted him back in my life! I thought of the many happy times we had spent together, and my dreams for our future. But then, despair would rear its ugly head, choking my dreams, like mesquite crowding out the prairie grass on Grandpa Thurmond's old grazing land.

Was it wrong to want him? If I had known he would react this way, would I have given him such an ultimatum? Or would I have entered into marriage with an unsaved man, and taken my chances that he would one day accept the Lord as his personal Savior? The Bible said I should not be unevenly yoked with an unbeliever. "What fellowship hath light with darkness?" And yet I missed him so!

Suppose he did call, and wanted to start dating again, without settling this issue? Could we ever be "just friends" again, or would it once again lead to a serious relationship?

In a town the size of Chaparral, it was inevitable that our paths would have to cross. What would I say to him?

* * *

Mama had asked me to drive to Perrin's Big Mart for some groceries. I entered the parking lot just as Dan loaded some bags into the trunk of his '48 Ford.

He looked as startled as I was, then walked toward me. I made no move to get out of the car, just sat there waiting. My hand shook as I rolled down the window.

He nodded. "You're looking good."

"You too."

I meant that, with all my heart. He looked wonderful. Even better than I had pictured him all these weeks, since the night of his proposal.

"I've got something to tell you," he said. "I thought about stopping over, but I wasn't sure I'd be welcome."

"You were the one that walked away, Dan."

"I couldn't be what you wanted, sweetheart. You deserve better."

"Dan, I. . ."

"I joined the army, Rosie."

"You did what?" My heart sank, as I processed the unbelievable news. "You're not serious! You've got school, and your job, and. . ."

"I am serious. I leave in two days for Fort Ord. And school is one of the reasons I'm doing it. Now that we're in peacetime, the G.I. Bill is a pretty good way to pay for college.

"I'm having trouble making ends meet, with tuition and books and utilities and all. It seemed like I was going to have to either cut out eating or quit turning my lights on to study by. And, now that my dad's not around, I don't need that big house anymore. I'm going to rent it out to a buddy of mine who's getting married."

And now that you and I aren't getting married, I

could almost hear him thinking.

I had really let Dan down. I hadn't even noticed the struggle he was having financially. That must be why he said we would have to wait to get married until he was done with this school year. If I had really loved him, I would have been more tuned in to what he was going through. Instead, I had been wrapped up in my own feelings.

"Two days?" I repeated, weakly. "I wish you would have told me."

"Well, I just did." He nodded again with a tight smile, and turned to hurry back to his car.

In the two days that followed, I could think of nothing else except that Dan would soon be on a plane that would fly him out of New Mexico, and that I may never see him again.

He hadn't asked me to go to the airport with him, or even said goodbye, really.

I went to the inn an hour before my shift was to begin that day, without even knowing why. I thought about talking to Mama about everything, but once I got there, I decided against it. This wasn't the right time or place.

At 4:30, I impulsively picked up the telephone and dialed the number for information. "The Tri-County Airport, please."

I dialed the number, my fingers trembling. "Do you have a flight leaving for California this evening, arriving near Fort Ord?"

"American Airlines Flight 49 departs at 6:10

p.m., Ma'am. That's at Gate 3B."

"Thank you."

That gave me just enough time to get Betsey to take my shift – Betsey would do it with no questions asked – and to make the 60-minute drive to the airport.

There was no time to think it through or ask myself any questions, about what good it would do or why I should go when he never even said he wanted me there.

Just before I pulled into the airport parking lot, it began to drizzle, and by the time I got out of the car it was truly raining. People were already coming out of the building at Gate 3B, about to board the waiting plane, and I saw Dan talking with two people who had come to see him off. I stayed back when they each gave him a big hug and quick kiss on the lips.

One was his older sister, Esther, and the other was my cousin, Carol Alverson. Carol was crying and whispering something into his ear. He turned to run, then, out of the rain and onto the stairway to board the plane. The women ran in the opposite direction.

I wasn't sure whether he saw me or not, but it did look like he may have glanced back, just as he reached the top of the stairs, with people coming up close behind him. I was too far back to call out his name, or to see him through the windows, but I stood and watched until the plane was completely out of sight, letting my teardrops fall with the rain now coming down in torrents.

***

One Sunday afternoon, Carol came into the inn as part of a dinner party for her father's birthday. When others in the party said hello and complimented the new decor in the dining room, I tried to speak cordially. I couldn't meet Carol's eyes. Ever since that night at the airport, when I had seen Dan kiss her, I had suspected that she had taken my place as his girlfriend. I didn't want to give her a chance to gloat.

Betsey had noticed this group as well. I had confided in her, and she knew I might be uncomfortable waiting on them. Just as I reached Carol's side of the table, Betsey greeted her and distracted her from whatever belittling remark she was about to say to me.

"Rosie, why don't you let me get the orders so you can help with the birthday cake?"

I squeezed her hand. Betsey was more than a cousin to me, she was a good friend.

Aunt Molly had the cake nearly finished, and I offered to put Uncle Thomas Quincy's name on it and set the candles in place. Betsey came in to pick it up, saying she would present it to them and I could wait on the next table.

I couldn't help wondering whether Carol really cared anything for Dan, or if she just relished the idea of taking him away from me. Somewhere in my heart, I still hoped Dan would eventually come to know the Lord, and there would be no more barriers to our getting married.

Carol's family stayed for the afternoon musical gathering that had been an Alverson tradition for so many years.

My heart wasn't in it these days, but I sang two of the old favorites, as usual, and stayed to listen as others joined in. I pretended to have a good time, determined to keep Carol from suspecting how deeply I missed Dan Cole.

At the end of my last song, I saw Denny Brewer with some friends, applauding me with more enthusiasm than my performance warranted and beckoning me to come and sit with them.

I didn't feel much like talking, but I made an effort to keep a smile on my face and listen attentively when Denny leaned over and whispered something in my ear. Life must go on, I reasoned, so I found myself agreeing to go bowling with him on my day off.

Later, I ran into Dan's older sister, Esther, coming out of the restroom.

"Rosie, can I talk to you for a minute?" she asked, pulling me over to a quiet corner.

"Dan wrote and told me he saw you out there, standing in the rain, when he was boarding the plane that day, but it was too late to go out and talk to you. He says he can't get his mind off you, and thinks he made a mistake by not asking you to see him off.

Could you write to him? He's so depressed right now. I think it would mean a lot to him."

"I don't know what good that would do," I said, fighting to hold back the tears welling up. "It's been more than two weeks since he left. I notice he didn't write me himself to ask me that. What's more, he had plenty of time to decide who he wanted to see him off. Maybe he should be asking her to cheer him up!"

"Well. . ." She thrust a slip of paper into my hand. "In case you change your mind, here's his address."

I put it into my skirt pocket and escaped into the restroom before I began to cry.

* * *

Mama had been trying to get me to "snap out of it" ever since I'd told her why Dan broke up with me, and why I turned down his proposal.

"You did the right thing, Rosie. Give yourself a chance to meet somebody who loves the Lord, like you do. Somewhere out there is a Christian man who is right for you."

I didn't tell her how hard it was for me to pray this past two months. What could I say to God? I had asked forgiveness for giving Dan the wrong impression, and for not being a better witness. Was I supposed to thank God that Dan was gone, when all of my zest for living seemed to have gone with him?

I longed to write to Dan, but I couldn't act as though everything was fine between us. I knew I had hurt him; I had let our relationship get too serious before I told him I could never marry an unbeliever. It was wrong to lead him on in the first place, but wouldn't I just be doing it again if I began a correspondence with him now?

* * *

It was Thursday afternoon. Denny Brewer would soon pick me up for bowling at Sunlight Lanes. I pulled on a terry cloth sweater, aqua to set off my trim white pants and tennies, knowing I would have to rent bowling shoes when I got there. This was to be the first time I had done anything on my day off in months.

Denny arrived with another couple, Ron and Doris, former classmates at Chaparral High. Denny looked cool and self-assured in his striped pullover and khaki denims, and his smile was contagious. He held the door open as I climbed into the front seat of his Olds convertible, thinking how glad I was I'd remembered to put a head scarf in my purse to keep my hair in place.

It was a real treat to be admired by a nice young man, with nothing expected of me except companionship for the day. Ron and Doris chatted in the back seat, and Denny interjected a witty remark now and then. Mostly we just enjoyed the ride and listened to the radio.

I found myself forgetting my troubles for a little while, and even laughed as my ball rolled into the gutter, and when Denny and Ron outdid each other in their showoff antics.

Denny took our friends home first, and then escorted me home, walking me to the door with his arm around my shoulders.

"I had a nice time," I told him.

"Okay if I call you once in awhile?"

"Sure. Goodnight, Denny."

"G'night, Rose."

That night, as I tossed and turned, I tried to hold on to recollections of the pleasant evening with Denny Brewer. But they were forced out by more unsettling memories of Dan Cole.

Why couldn't I fall in love with someone like Denny? Couldn't he be that special someone the Lord wanted me to spend my future with? It would be so much simpler, if I could transfer my feelings to Dennis. I knew he loved the Lord; we attended the same church; he was preparing for a good job as a pharmacist in his father's store, and maybe taking over someday.

If he was the right man for me, why didn't his absence turn my life upside down, or his presence make me feel as though I was already his life-long partner? I had known Dennis as long as I had known Dan, maybe longer. Wouldn't I have known by now if there could be anything but casual friendship between us?

Oh, Lord, I prayed. *If a meaningful relationship with Denny is the path You would have me follow, please help me to know it – to feel something stronger and deeper than casual fondness for him.*

I knew that emotions were not all that counted in a major decision, like choosing a marriage partner, but surely a woman must bring love and devotion for her spouse if she is to be a good wife and mother?

* * *

As hard as it was to get Dan off my mind, I never wrote to Dan, and apparently Carol did.

I was crushed by a brief, accidental meeting months later at the dime store. My heart had missed a beat, seeing him suddenly, standing in the checkout line; and then I saw that Carol was there, by his side. All I could think of at that moment was that his incredible good looks were even more outstanding with a deep tan against the light, khaki uniform he wore.

He looked a little uncomfortable, but he said "Hello," and Carol just smiled. A weak wave and a half-smile was all I could manage, and I left the store quickly.

Until that day, I had secretly held onto some hope that Dan would somehow return to me, get right with the Lord, and marry me. Now, seeing that he was spending his leave with Carol, I lost any hope for that.

Oh, Lord, I prayed that night, once I had shed every tear that had been building up inside me. *I don't know what You have in mind for my future. Help me to trust You more, and know that Your will is best.* I fell asleep feeling more at peace than I had in months.

* * *

Someone once said that time heals all wounds. But even though the seasons changed, and special events came and went – Janet's and Thomas' weddings, Margaret and Derron's first child, Christmas and all of the other holidays with my family – time alone could never have gotten me through one year, and then another, since my heart had been broken.

It was God's love that carried me, and made me realize at last that there was joy, in spite of everything, because true joy depended on my relationship with Him, not on my circumstances.

Spending just a little more time in His Word and a little less time in self-pity, I began to grow as a more mature Christian at last.

CHAPTER 17

"You missed a good service tonight," my brother Tim said one Sunday evening as he came back from church.

"I meant to go tonight to hear that guest speaker," I said. "I couldn't get away in time, though. They were short-handed at the inn. Was he pretty good?"

"Oh, yeah, he was great. Several people went to the altar tonight – including Carol Alverson."

I almost spilled the coffee I had just poured, I was so surprised.

"Carol?" The news startled me. I was speechless. "Praise the Lord!" I finally managed to say.

That night, before climbing into bed, I went on my knees for a prayer of thanks.

My prayers had been answered. With God's help, I had learned not to carry bitterness toward anybody, but nothing else could possibly have changed my view of Carol so dramatically.

I saw her now, in my mind's eye, not as a hard-hearted socialite, bent on making my life miserable, but as a lost soul who needed the Lord, just like the rest of us. And now, without any helpful word from me, she had found Him.

I wanted earnestly to befriend her and encourage her in her new walk with the Lord. I even accepted the possibility that Carol and Dan might care deeply for one another, and that, if it was God's will, I would graciously stay out of the way.

***

The annual Sunday school picnic began at 11 a.m. on Saturday. I really wanted to go, so I found someone to take my place at the inn.

It was one of the occasions for Christian fellowship that I always looked forward to. It gave us all a chance to get to know the new members while mixing with old friends at the same time.

Even Carol's presence gave me pleasure today, something I would have once thought impossible, had it not been for the surprising news about her trip to the altar a month ago. Today, I felt a deep concern for her, as she walked around in silence.

Her eyes looked uneasy, until they met mine and saw that my smile was genuine. She immediately smiled back, and approached me.

"Good to see you here!" I said, knowing she would need encouragement, now that she was seeing everything with new eyes.

"I've been looking forward to it. I'm glad you could get off work for a while. It's a beautiful day to be out, isn't it?"

Then, without either of us seeming to know how it happened, my arms went around her. Lightly. Gently. And Carol responded with a warm hug. Then we turned and joined the others in enjoying the day.

Later, Carol and I talked again while we helped set out the food. Dennis Brewer had arrived, and just as he greeted us both, someone called him over to help move some tables. Then Carol asked me, cautiously, whether Denny and I were engaged.

"Denny and I? Oh, no! We're just friends who've known each other forever."

When I saw her trying to hold back a smile of relief, I looked over at Denny and back at Carol, in sudden realization that she may have more than a mild curiosity on the subject.

Carol continued to watch him work, and then blushed slightly when Denny looked her way briefly and waved.

"So you wouldn't mind if I invited him to go riding with me sometime?"

"Of course not! I'm sure he'd be really pleased if you did. But I am a little surprised that you're interested. I mean, I thought maybe you and Dan had a serious understanding."

She smiled. "Dan and I are good friends. I write to him a lot because he doesn't seem to have anybody. No family, even, except his sister Esther." She paused. "He's never gotten over you, you know."

I found myself explaining to her why I had turned down Dan's proposal of marriage, even though I had wanted to say yes.

"I'm afraid I hurt him much more than I should have, but I just didn't think it would work since he didn't share my love for the Lord."

"Rosemary, didn't you know that Dan was saved nearly a year ago? He's the one who's been witnessing to me all this time!"

I felt my spirits rise for the first time since Dan joined the army. My eyes turned toward heaven. I praised God in silence.

All of the love for Dan that I had been trying to hold inside came rising to the surface, flooding my heart with tender memories that I'd been afraid to dwell on in the past two years.

I had forgiven Dan and Carol at last, for what I thought was a love affair. Still, I should have tried to remain Dan's friend, to at least be willing to write him occasionally. It was just that thinking of him at all still hurt. I hadn't given much thought to how I might be hurting him.

For the next few days, I prayed about it, repenting for whatever pride or unkind thoughts had kept me from writing him.

And then I took out a fresh sheet of stationery and began my first letter to Dan.

Dear Dan,

It has been so long since we've talked, and it's hard to know what to say to you.

I am especially sorry for any pain that I have caused you in the past, and for not having been kind enough to write you during your service to our country. It was selfish and inconsiderate.

The Lord, in His mercy, is helping me recognize these failings, and I hope you will forgive me for them, as He has.

I have heard that you have come to Christ, and I rejoice with you as a sister in the faith.

The times we shared together will always be special to me. Please know that I miss you and would love to hear from you if you care to write.

Love,
Rosemary Alverson

Dan's reply from California arrived five days later. The sight of his familiar handwriting on the envelope sent a thrill into the deepest part of my heart, and sustained me until I could go to my room and read it in privacy.

Dear Rosemary;

I hope I will someday find the right words to tell you how much your letter meant to me.

God is so good, Rosie. He forgave me for all those years of doubting Him. Since I finally came to know Him as my Lord and Savior, He's taught me to forgive others as well – even my father. As for causing pain, I'm sure my abrupt departure, without even saying a proper goodbye, must have hurt you as much as you hurt me. You certainly didn't deserve that.

I will have another leave coming in about six weeks. Then, when I come back, I will only have four months to go before my discharge.

Please say you'll meet me at the airport when I come? I'll let you know when I get my exact schedule. Meanwhile, I'll be watching my mailbox for more of your precious letters.

Love Always,
Dan Cole

CHAPTER 18

I wrote Dan nearly every night, not even waiting for a response before I wrote another. Reading his letters became the high point of my day, and I read each one over and over.

I couldn't wait for Dan to come home. I had no doubt, now, that he was the love of my life. Now that we had our faith in common, I wanted nothing more than to marry Dan, have babies, raise them together, and live happily ever after.

If I bore Dan's children, what would they look like? I tried to imagine little girls who looked a little like me, and boys with Dan's heavy eyelids, sturdy jaws and barrel chests, like miniature football players.

I knew they wouldn't inherit Dan's scarred upper lip. That had happened when he fell, as a ten-year-old, down some stairs which had been poorly constructed by my ancestors. To me, it just enhanced the face I loved so dearly.

Would any of our children inherit my grandmother's red hair or the fair, freckled complexion that came from both sides of my family? Or would they have chestnut brown, unruly locks like my mother and I?

What kind of a wife would I be?

I knew I was rushing things to be thinking of marriage. Wasn't Dan planning on going off to finish college, using his G.I. Bill benefits to pursue his goal to become a teacher? Suppose he met someone else while he was in college?

Perhaps he would get a job offer from a faraway place. Would I be willing to leave my family and friends to be with him? I knew the answer to that. Just as my great-grandmother Elizabeth followed Grandpa Thurmond to New Mexico, I would be happy to follow Dan anywhere the Lord led him.

Maybe he is worried we wouldn't have enough money. I knew Dan wouldn't be able to earn much while he went to college, but I could work, too, at least until we started a family. *We don't need a fancy house,* I would tell him. *We just need each other.*

So, what would I do if he didn't repeat his proposal? I thought of my Aunt Lou, who had gotten tired of waiting for Uncle Tommy, and "popped the question" herself.

If he doesn't bring it up while he's home, I determined, *I will!*

***

As people came out of the plane and down the steps, I could not help remembering the night I stood here in this very spot, helplessly watching, with the rain beating against my face.

But, this time, Dan had asked me to come, and before I even spotted him, my legs were threatening to give way beneath me.

There he was, at last! His searching eyes lit up when they found me. I nearly cried out in excitement as he ran towards me. Seconds later he had gathered me in his arms. Then came a long, warm kiss, right there in the airport, and a moment of laughter, because we both had tears in our eyes. Hand in hand, we went to retrieve his luggage, and headed out to the parking lot.

Out in my car, we kissed again.

"I'm so sorry about everything, Rosemary." Dan's voice dropped down to a low, rich tone, which made me feel like the most desirable woman in the world. "I don't ever want to lose you again."

On the way back to Chaparral, we talked about our old school friends. He asked about my family, and how my work at the inn was going. I asked him about army life, and laughed as he described some of his buddies' practical jokes. We'd already written most of the news in our letters, but I loved hearing the sound of his voice. To have him actually here, in person, felt so good, he could have been reciting the Gettysburg Address and I would have enjoyed listening to him.

"How much did they feed you on the plane? If you're hungry, we could go get a meal at the inn. Swiss steak is the special today."

"Sounds great. They never feed you on these shorter flights."

As we turned onto Alverson Drive, he asked me

to take him to his old house, first. "I want to drop off my rucksack and check on the place. Besides, we could use some time alone," he added. "You don't have to work today, do you?"

I shook my head, smiling impishly. "No sir! I'm taking my annual vacation this week. I'm hoping to spend it with somebody special!

Pulling into Dan's driveway, I couldn't help noticing that his expression turned more serious.

"Look at me, Rosemary," Dan implored me softly and waited for me to comply.

I'd never seen a man look the way Dan looked at that moment. He faced me now with tender determination, and I held back the tears I felt gathering behind my eyes. He reached for me and drew me closer.

"Let's not ever let it happen again, Rose. Not ever! We belong together. You know that, don't you?"

Dan watched my eyes intently and waited until I nodded, with a tear rolling down my cheek. He drew me close now, whispering through my hair, holding me and rocking me in his strong, tender arms. Then he pulled back a little and reached into a pocket for something he was trying to show me.

Releasing me from his embrace, he held out a black velvet box and opened it, displaying a small but beautiful diamond ring.

"Please say you'll marry me, sweetheart?"

"Of course," I whispered. And then, unsure if he

had understood my response through the deep sobs in my throat, I tried again.

"Yes. Absolutely yes! I'll marry you whenever you say!" He slipped the ring on my finger, and then my tears turned to quiet, joyful laughter, as he grabbed me and drew me close again, kissing my face, my nose, my chin, and then hugging me tightly once more.

When finally we just sat quietly in each other's embrace, Dan spoke again.

"Whenever I say. That's the hard part, honey."

He stroked my cheek with his strong hands, and looked into my inquiring eyes.

"I've been trying to figure out what's best. When I get my discharge, in four months, I'll want you with me, but I'll have nothing to offer you, at all.

"Any job I could get without a college education would barely keep food on the table and a roof over our heads. Rent and utilities are expensive. And how would we ever be able to start a family? But if I get back in college on the GI Bill, I can only work part-time, at the most. Do you want to wait three more years?"

"No! But, I'm working full time now, at the inn. I've even saved a little, living at home. We could make it!"

"Oh, I've saved a little too. About enough to buy some old car to go back and forth to school in! If I ever get back in school, that is."

"Of course you'll go back to school!" I said without hesitation.

"We could manage one of the low-income apartments downtown, just on my earnings, Dan. My parents would probably let me work more hours, if I asked them. We could pick up some second-hand furniture at the thrift store, and I know we'd get most of our small stuff as wedding gifts."

"When would we ever see each other then? I'd have my part-time work and studies, and you'd be at the inn at most mealtimes! We should probably wait."

My heart sank. We had been so happy, so elated, not half an hour ago, and now it sounded as though we would have to wait for years.

"Let me bring in my stuff, and we'll talk some more." I went in with him, and we entered through the weather-worn back door.

I'd been in the Cole house once before with my brother Tim, after the funeral for Dan's mother. Maynard was still living then. Tim had told me that any attempt to keep the old house up was made by Dan himself, between school and work on the ranch. The old man, Dan said, had lost some of his meanness after his mother died, but spent most of his last days in her old rocking chair, staring into space, and wearing the same overalls and tee-shirt every day with no inclination to let his son launder them.

Now the house lay empty, smelling of mildew

and probably taken over by mice and cockroaches while Dan had been away. Even Dan's friend had decided not to rent it after he saw the shape it was in.

I looked around, trying to picture the family who lived here for so many years. Dan had told me his oldest brother, Everett, had run off the day after he finished high school and never contacted them again. The second oldest, Alton, had died in Korea. Esther had married at 16 to a man twice her age, just to get away from home. Dan the youngest, ended up taking care of his parents in their last years.

Flour-sack curtains hung limply on makeshift wire rods. A stained, 1930-style sink had never been replaced, and the badly worn couch and over-stuffed chair sat on worn linoleum. Moisture from a leaky roof had trailed down the papered walls, and had rotted a patch of rough-boarded floor in one corner of the dining area.

"Dan, did you know that one of my daddy's uncles built this house?"

"That's what I heard from your brother Tim. He wasn't much of a carpenter."

"Too much in a hurry, I think. But ten years later, he built the one next to ours. That's pretty solid, so I guess he had learned from somebody."

An idea circled around in my head and I just had to express it.

"Does this house belong to you, now?"

"Well, it's half mine. I can live in it, and if I sell it, Esther gets half the proceeds. But who would want to buy it?"

"Couldn't we live in it? No mortgage payment, right?"

He grimaced. "I could live in it, but I made up my mind a long time ago that my wife would never have to live the way my mother did!"

"It would be temporary, Dan, just like it was for the people who built it! We could fix it up a little, but it doesn't have to be perfect. We'll have each other, and we'll make it into a home, for now."

"I don't know, honey. This place is really a dump. I don't mind it for myself, but I want so much better for you!"

"It'll be a start for us, and a challenge! We won't have to wait, and we'll get something else when we're ready. Let's do it!"

In my mind's eye, I could see it transformed into a tidy little home, with frilly curtains and morning glories twining around the windows – truly a honeymoon cottage.

He finally agreed that it would solve our initial budget problems, and I took one last look at the worn-out interior before we left.

We'll make it do, I resolved silently.

Butt You will be here, too, won't You, Lord?

CHAPTER 19

Dan went back to Fort Ord just before Valentine's Day, in 1957, leaving me to plan our June wedding, get the house ready, and work as many hours as my parents would allow to help pay for needed repairs.

He would be home two weeks before the big day, so he would start right away applying by mail to re-enroll in the university, and lining up a part-time job.

I envisioned frilly curtains and brightly colored throw rugs over re-varnished floors. I did not realize how bad the roof leaked, or how crooked the rough-hewn floorboards were under that old linoleum. My brother Tim had offered to help me get rid of the rodent-inhabited couch and chair, and discard the old floor covering.

As it turned out, I was faced with the decision between either replacing the entire floor or covering it with plywood and then installing either carpeting or new asphalt tiles. I could not afford carpeting, so I opted for the plywood and some of the new asphalt tiles over the entire living and dining-room area.

The tiles only came in three colors: black with white streaks, white with black streaks, or chocolate brown with red streaks. So I chose the chocolate brown for the living room-dining area and a black and white checkerboard pattern for the kitchen. This project used up most of my savings, even though Tim donated his labor.

"Rosie," my brother began, as I watched him nailing down the plywood one day, "you're going to have to do something with that roof, or all this work will be a waste of time."

We couldn't afford a whole new roof. Tim and Thomas crawled up there one day and figured out what they would have to do to stop the leaks, and I was dismayed to see the cost figures they came up with for that.

I went home to get ready for work, and to my delight, a letter from Dan included a money order, which, as he explained, was meant for roof repairs. I had not wanted to bother him with financial worries in my letters to him, partly because I wanted to surprise him with the new look of his old house when he came home. But he knew the place well, and what minimal repairs would be essential to make it livable for the woman he loved.

The heavy, round table, made of light oak with maple-colored finish, was in fair condition, but every one of the six chairs needed new upholstery covering. I decided to tackle this task myself, using a deep blue shade of brocade that I found on sale. I bought enough extra fabric to make matching draperies for the two dining room windows.

I found some ivy-patterned wallpaper for the kitchen, and paint for the dining room. I decided to try Mama's old technique, from the Elm Street house, painting the dining room with cream-colored paint, and using a piece of sponge to apply feathery blobs of sky blue when it was dry.

For the living room, I found some wallpaper that had the look – but not the cost – of mahogany paneling. I used it on one wall, and some amber wallpaper with tiny white flowers for the remaining walls, to avoid a dark, gloomy appearance in the room.

The main source of frustration, as I applied all of this lovely paper, was that none of the walls were truly straight. The job required quite a lot of piecing, and I hoped nobody would come close enough to see the many flaws.

How strange, I thought, that this hurriedly-built home had stood for fifty years, and yet, at close range, resembled a house of cards that was about to collapse. But, Dan, I discovered, was almost a perfectionist in anything he set his hand to. In his high school shop class, he had built work counters for his mother, the Christmas before she died.

The corners were flawlessly formed to make a convenient U-shaped work area. The countertop resembled finished pine, and had a bright linoleum back-splash and a narrow metal trim. Dan had planned to replace the old sink as soon as he could save enough money. But his mother did not live to see another Christmas, or to long enjoy the improvements her son was trying to make in her bleak existence.

All three bedrooms were upstairs, accessible only by climbing the same steep, rickety stairway down which ten-year-old Dan had fallen, face first, creating the disfiguring scar he would carry all his life.

In one bedroom was a four-poster bed, which was so heavy, nobody would ever get it out of the room without breaking it into pieces. Two tattered mattresses on old-fashioned bed springs made it higher than normal, and would require low stools at either side of the bed to climb into. A matching dresser, with a tall mirror behind it, appeared to be serviceable. I would just replace the rotting curtains, and the faded wallpaper in all three bedrooms would have to wait.

Now we were only lacking some living room furniture. I had run out of money in my savings account, and now my weekly savings would have to be set aside for wedding expenses.

I would be the fourth daughter that my daddy would "marry off", and I knew that the custom had been established, starting with Margaret's wedding, that they would provide only what they could afford to do for all of us. This consisted of a wedding gown, a cake, and a generous supply of punch for the guests. We would be married at our church, of course, and could have the reception at the inn.

Any other "frills" would be the responsibility of the bride and groom.

This meant Dan and I would need to pay for all of the flowers, invitations, photography, candlesticks, and centerpieces. Food, aside from the cake, would have to be kept simple, and the guest list must not get out of hand.

I decided to have just two attendants – Betsey as a bridesmaid, and my sister Janet as matron of honor. Dan wrote, in response to my inquiry, that he'd like my brother Tim as his best man, and a school friend of his as a groomsman.

Mama and Aunt Molly took me to buy fabric for my wedding gown. Betsey and Janet went along to look for patterns for their dresses, which would be made in the yellow, antique satin that I liked. Each of the men, including the groom, would be wearing a soft brown suit, which they could then continue to wear on Sunday, dressed up with antique satin vests made of the same soft yellow as the ladies' dresses.

"My mama will decorate the cake," Betsey announced on the way to the bridal shop. "Your mother will bake it and make all of the frosting, and then my mama will do all the yellow roses the way you like them." Aunt Molly had always been the official cake decorator for the family.

Dan was flabbergasted when he walked in and saw what we'd done to the house. There was even a couch by then, because the family had voted to purchase a new one for the lobby and had given us the old one, still in good condition. It was in a floral print with a pale tan background, and western style wooden arms.

By the time Dan came home, there had been two bridal showers; my aunts had hosted a large one at the inn, from which we received every kind of up-to-date utensil, small appliance and unbreakable place setting a household of the fifties could have wanted, and towels and bedding to last for years; and then a small, personal shower was held in Betsey's apartment downtown. That day, four of my close friends, with my mother and sisters, gave me negligees and both under and outer clothing to wear on the honeymoon, although I didn't yet know where that would be.

We had the invitations in the mail, the gowns made, and I'd settled on chicken sandwiches, baked beans, a green salad, and potato chips to feed reception guests.

The only change Dan made to the menu was to add his favorite: ground bologna, formed in the shape of a pig by his friend's mother. He bought the ingredients for this, and provided a platter of split buns to put beside it on the table.

Our wedding could not have gone more smoothly, in spite of the frantic pace of the last-minute preparations.

My cousin Rachel played the organ, and my sister Carrie sang "I Love You Truly." Daddy's cousin, my "Uncle Todd," and Aunt Melissa served as Master and Mistress of Ceremonies.

As Dan and I pledged our love and faithfulness to one another at the altar, I felt that Heaven itself had opened up, and all the angels were smiling down on our union.

***

The honeymoon was Dan's surprise for me. We spent our wedding night in our newly-refurbished home, and two days and nights in Tucumcari. There was a motor court there with a romantic honeymoon cabin, boasting room service and piped-in music, and quaint little shops and cafes nearby.

I had been a little worried about spending our first night at home. Some of our friends might play embarrassing "chivaree" pranks on us. But Dan had come up with a way to throw them off.

He had purchased a second old car for him to use, driving to and from the university, but had not yet brought it home.

So, we left the reception in my car, which had been decorated with tin cans and balloons. We went to the Auto Mart, parked behind the building, and switched cars. Then we drove quietly to Old Alverson Lane and parked down the road from our house. We ran across the road and slipped in the back door, stifling our laughter and shushing each other.

Dan had left soft night lights on in every room, so we wouldn't have to turn on the main lights. Besides maintaining our privacy, the effect was quite romantic.

I let him use the bathroom first, and he came out wearing a new pair of blue silk pajamas. He kissed me, and left a faint taste of toothpaste on my lips.

"I won't be long," I tried to say brightly, as I ducked into the bathroom to put on one of my new, filmy nightgowns.

Moments later, Dan led me up the narrow stairs to where the four-poster bed had been laid with fresh linens and a new coverlet.

"Nervous?" he asked, as the door of the tiny room creaked shut behind us.

"A little." It was an understatement. My heart was beating wildly.

Then he did a wonderful thing. He took my hand and, instead of climbing immediately into bed, he went down on his knees beside it, pulling me gently to kneel beside him.

He bowed his head and prayed. "Heavenly Father, thank you for giving me this lovely, Christian woman to wed. Please help me to be the kind of husband you want me to be, and bless our union, now and forever."

Now, any trepidation that I had felt was gone. I pulled back the covers and climbed in, holding out my arms to the man I would spend forever with. There, as the full moon cast its soft light on our faces, my husband kissed me with a soft-sweet urgency that took my breath away.

***

Dawn crept through the window in slow, quiet stages, reminding me that I lay there, still, in my husband's arms, unwilling to move from his gentle embrace. At last I was right here at his side, where I belonged.

I lay in silent prayer until I felt his arms move, pulling me even closer as though to make sure I was still there. Snuggling lazily against his chest, I smiled at the low sigh of contentment just before his eyes opened, heavy-lidded and searching for my lips, on which he planted the first kiss of the day.

"Good morning, Mrs. Cole." A sleepy smile brought mine in response.

"Good morning, Mr. Cole. I love you!"

"How'd I ever get a beautiful gal like you to marry me? I'll be glad when we get some daylight in here, so I can see if it's really you!"

I pretended to try to swat him for saying that, and he grabbed my wrists, playfully, and planted another kiss on my laughing lips. Then I returned it in earnest.

An hour later we got up, looked around for our clothes, and remembered we had left our luggage downstairs.

Again, I let him use the bathroom first, while I picked out my clothes for the day - a white terry cloth sports outfit with red trim.

"No use unpacking anything yet. We'll be leaving right after breakfast," he called. When he came out, tiny droplets from the shower were shining on his suntanned shoulders.

I took my shower and got dressed, meeting the smell of coffee and bacon when I stepped into the dining room. Finding Dan moving fried eggs from a sizzling pan onto his old, china plates, I hoped he didn't think I was unable or unwilling to cook his breakfast.

The toast popped up from our new automatic Sunbeam, and I buttered it while he took up the bacon.

I didn't tell him that I preferred my eggs sunny side up, and my bacon a little bit crispier. I knew we would both have much to learn about each other, and would also need to make some adjustments.

We cleaned up the kitchen together, and began to load up for the trip. Apparently, nobody had suspected that we had spent our wedding night right there in our own home.

CHAPTER 20

The day we returned from Tucumcari, my mother reminded me that we still needed to pick up our gifts from the storage room at the inn. We still had a small mountain of shower gifts stacked in our living room.

Dan said he would prefer to tackle this project yet today, because he was due to start one of his new jobs in the morning.

Margaret had made a list showing who gave us what, for the thank you cards I would need to send. So we decided that a good first step would be to examine all the gifts and place them in categories before attempting to put them away.

This turned out to be fun for both of us. We had been overwhelmed with the gift opening ritual at the reception, oohing and ahing over each delightful item and locating, with our smiling gaze, each giver. It was nice, now, to have more time to look at each one.

A small tower of soft, new towel sets in pastel colors took up one end of our dining table. Bed linens and blankets filled the rest of it.

Mama and Daddy had given us silverware, with a sleek, swirling pattern, and serving utensils to match. The aunts and uncles had gone in together to order a full set of china dishes with my favorite yellow roses, and Aunt Molly had pointed out that if ever a piece was broken, we could replace it by using the number on the bottom of the dish.

My three sisters and their spouses had chipped in to buy a large wall clock, which chimed every hour and sent out a little peasant girl and boy figurine to greet us.

Every kitchen utensil and tablecloth, dishtowel and potholder had been chosen with care and offered in love, to make our home extra-special.

We stopped to enjoy a cup of coffee, giving ourselves time to admire our new things, treasuring them mostly because now they belonged to the two of us, together.

The next day, Dan went off to his stable-cleaning job and I kept busy at home, having taken the entire week off.

Most of the house had been thoroughly cleaned long before our wedding day, but there was still more to do.

The old gas range still needed a good cleaning. It was similar to the old Magic Chef stove my mother had used when I was small, back in Michigan. It stood on legs, and had four black burners, which, like the oven, had to be lighted with a match – carefully, because it ignited with a sudden flare when it finally came on. But it still worked, and, as Dan had pointed out, his Mama had turned out wonderful baked goods every day with that stove.

I wore rubber gloves, like Aunt Lou did at the Inn, but, careful as I was, I still got black gunk all over my brand new apron before I was finished. And the fumes were terrible.

I wasn't able to get the brown stains out of that old sink, although I scoured it with Old Dutch Cleanser. At least I was able to polish the faucets a little.

I wiped off the small refrigerator, which had a tiny freezer compartment just large enough to hold two ice cube trays. It would need defrosting much more often, it turned out, than those at the inn. Otherwise, the eggs and milk would freeze, and the lettuce would be hard as a rock.

I sat down and looked around our little home. Even after all the improvements, it certainly wasn't fancy. Those rickety stairs were still treacherous. The roof would probably develop more leaks, and dust had already begun to blow through the gaps in the window sills, accumulating on my polished furniture.

But this was our home – mine and Dan's. I knew I couldn't be any happier if we lived in a palace. Maybe it was just knowing that, here, I had begun sharing the rest of my life with the man I loved and respected.

That was all I wanted.

Coming in 2013

**Uncover the mystery surrounding
the ancestors of
Rosemary, Margaret and Matilda in
Echoes of Elizabeth
fourth in the series
Hearts in Harmony
by Marcella Taylor Hoffman**

READERS – Please tell us…

What did you most enjoy about this story?

What kind of stories you would like to read in the future

Personal comments for the author

Your age group
___10 to 20 ___20 to 40 ___40 to 60 ___Over 60

___Please notify me of new books by this (publisher) (author)
by E-Mail _____
or at this address_____
_____
_____

Return this page to Golden Apple Greetings, 5066 Lake Michigan Drive, Allendale, MI 49401

Or e-mail the author at taylorshug.8@hotmail.com